Venture into this dungeon . . .

. . . and you will discover a Chinese dragon who lives on a roof; alien beasts wandering round a village; a huge sea serpent of classical legend; a terrible, wild, grey, hairy thing and many other funny or fearsome monsters. You won't want to stop reading till you've tunnelled right out of the dungeon!

Every story in this dungeon is a tried and tested favourite, ideal for reading aloud at bedtime or in the classroom, or for older readers to tackle alone. The selection features stories from such top children's authors as Joan Aiken, Adèle Geras and Terry Jones.

www.booksattransworld.co.uk/childrens

A Dungeon Full of Monster Stories

Collected by Pat Thomson

Illustrated by Peter Bailey

CORGI BOOKS

A DUNGEON FULL OF MONSTER STORIES
A CORGI BOOK : 0 552 545430

First publication in Great Britain

PRINTING HISTORY
Corgi edition published 2001

1 3 5 7 9 10 8 6 4 2

Set in 16/20pt Bembo Schoolbook by
Phoenix Typesetting, Ilkley, West Yorkshire

Corgi Books are published by Transworld Publishers,
61–63 Uxbridge Road, London W5 5SA,
a division of The Random House Group Ltd,
in Australia by Random House Australia (Pty) Ltd,
20 Alfred Street, Milsons Point, Sydney, NSW 2061, Australia,
in New Zealand by Random House New Zealand Ltd,
18 Poland Road, Glenfield, Auckland 10, New Zealand
and in South Africa by Random House (Pty) Ltd,
Endulini, 5a Jubilee Road, Parktown 2193, South Africa

Printed and bound in Great Britain by
Cox & Wyman Ltd, Reading, Berkshire

Acknowledgements

The editor and publisher are grateful for permission
to include the following copyright stories:

'The Liquorice Tree', from *The Winter Sleepwalker* by
Joan Aiken originally published by Jonathan Cape.
Used by permission of The Random House Group
Limited © Joan Aiken/1994.

Adèle Geras, 'Beauty and the Beast', from *Beauty
and the Beast and other Stories* (Hamish Hamilton,
1996). Reprinted by permission of Penguin Books Ltd.

Robert Hull, 'Finn mac Cumaill', from *Tales Around
the World* (Wayland, 1994). Reprinted by permission
of Hodder and Stoughton Limited.

Terry Jones, 'The Dragon in the Roof', from *Fantastic
Stories* (Pavilion, 1992). Reprinted by permission of
Pavilion Books.

Robin Klein, 'Thing' (Oxford University Press,
1982). Reprinted by permission from Hodder
Children's Books Australia.

Janet McNeill, 'Miss Hegarty and the Beastie'.
Reprinted by permission of A.P. Watt Ltd on behalf
of David Alexander.

Margaret Nash, 'Julie Parker's Enormous Secret',
from *Enough is Enough* (Viking Kestrel, 1989).
Reprinted by permission of the author.

James Riordan, 'Perseus and Andromeda', from
The Story Telling Star (Pavilion, 1999). Reprinted by
permission of Pavilion.

Dinah Starkey, 'The Draiglin' Hogney', from
Ghosts and Bogles (Heinemann, 1978). Reprinted by
permission of the author.

Pat Thomson, 'The Seven Monsters', © Pat Thomson,
2001. Reprinted by permission of the author.

Every effort has been made to trace and contact copyright
holders before publication. If any errors or omissions occur
the publisher will be pleased to rectify these at the earliest
opportunity.

Contents

The Draiglin' Hogney

There was once a lord who had three sons. Fine brave young men they were, with blood as blue as ink and hearts as bold as lions. But they hadn't two pennies to rub together because their father had fallen on hard times and all their land was gone.

So the eldest brother decided to seek his fortune and he set off one day with his hawk and his hound and his white Arab charger. And he rode and he rode till he'd left his own country far behind him and he was in a land he'd never seen before. A dark forest stretched ahead of him and leading into the forest was a narrow track. It looked a strange, lonely sort of place, but the young man was looking for adventure so he turned his horse and rode on.

But it was very still under the trees and no sun shone. Even the birds were silent and the leaves seemed to be whispering to each other. The hound slunk along with its tail between its legs and the horse set its ears back and shied at every step.

After a while the quiet and the dark began to get the young man down too, and he was sickening for voices and company. Then, through the trees, he saw lights glinting.

He spurred the horse on and soon they came to a great clearing. Within it stood a palace, glittering with gold and silver and precious stones. The garden was set with fountains and flowering trees, and there were lights blazing at every window, but there wasn't a soul to be seen.

The young man knocked on the gate and it swung open, though no hand moved it. The horse could hardly be persuaded inside. He went on into the palace, while the hound whined and shivered. The floors were of marble and the horse's hooves rang out hard and loud.

He came at last to a great banqueting hall. A feast was laid out on gold and silver plates. There was roast pig and peacock and marzipan trifles, and the wine, which stood in tall silver flagons, was the finest he'd ever tasted. Food was laid out for the beasts, too – hay for the horse and meat for the hound and hawk. They were all very tired so they set to and ate and drank their fill.

It was very late by now and they were just settling down to go to sleep when the clock struck twelve. On the last stroke the doors were flung open and into the hall strode the Draiglin' Hogney.

At the very sight of him, the dog's hackles rose, the horse reared and the hawk bated like a mad thing. But the young man, who was a kindly soul, said cheerfully, 'I suppose we've got you to thank for our supper. Pull up a chair.'

The Draiglin' Hogney made a horrible attempt at a smile and sat down by the fire. He looked at the furious beasts and said abruptly, 'Does your hound bite?'

'Well . . .' said the young man, rather taken aback. 'Sometimes.'

'Throw this over him,' said the Draiglin' Hogney 'That'll cure him.'

He passed the young man a long hair and the eldest son, bewildered but polite, laced it into the hound's collar.

'It's very kind . . .' he began, but the Draiglin' Hogney barked, 'And does your horse kick?'

'From time to time,' said the young man, baffled.

'Take this.'

He handed over another hair and the young man bound it into the horse's bridle.

'Does your hawk rend?'

'I wouldn't say *rend* exactly . . .'

'Does she or doesn't she? Yes or no?'

'Yes,' said the young man.

'Here.'

He produced a third hair which the young man twisted into the hawk's jesses.

'I really am most grateful,' he said.
'And after we've come in and eaten all
your food too. But I don't think I know
your name.'

'I,' said his host, 'am the Draiglin'
Hogney.' His voice rose to a roar and
all his whiskers bristled. 'And when a
stranger comes to my house, he never
gets out alive!'

With that he whipped out a slim
magician's rod and pointed it at the
young man. The hound strained
forward, the hawk screamed and the
horse slashed with his hooves, but the
hairs tightened round them like chains
and they were held fast. As for the
young man, he fell senseless to the floor
and that was the last thing he knew.

His father and two brothers waited
and waited for the eldest son to return.
But spring and summer went by and
still he didn't come back. So the middle

brother decided to go in search of the first and took his horse and his hound and his hawk and rode off till he too came to the forest and the deserted palace. He ate his fill in the banqueting hall and had just settled down to sleep when midnight struck and the Draiglin' Hogney appeared.

Now the second brother was just as friendly as the first and he saw nothing wrong with the Draiglin' Hogney, even if he did have fangs hanging down to his chest. He paid no heed to the snarls of his hound or the screams of his hawk and he bound them all up with the magic hairs.

But then the Draiglin' Hogney laughed horribly and cried, 'Your brother is already in my power and now I have you too!' and he pointed his magician's staff and the middle brother fell to the floor senseless. And though the animals screamed with fury, the hairs held them in and they were helpless.

The third son waited alone with his father until it was plain his brothers would not return. Then he took *his* horse and his hound and his hawk and set off in his turn. He found the forest all right but, being a careful man by nature, would have skirted it. But then it occurred to him that it was the very place for an adventure so, knowing his brothers, he rode in.

He came to the palace and the banqueting hall where the feast lay ready. Though he was very hungry, he wouldn't touch a crumb because he decided the whole place reeked of magic and he had no wish to be turned into a toad. So he made his supper off a bit of bread and cheese of his own bringing and settled down to wait.

Sure enough, midnight struck and the Draiglin' Hogney appeared. Now the youngest brother was friendly all right, but he was nobody's fool and he spotted the fangs straight away, *and* the long sharp claws, too. But he greeted his host pleasantly enough and they settled down by the fire for a chat.

'Does your horse kick?' demanded the Draiglin' Hogney.

'No,' said the young man, promptly. 'Never.'

'Liar!' cried the Draiglin' Hogney. 'There isn't a horse on earth that never kicks.'

'Mine doesn't.'

'Humph! Well, you're to wrap this round his bridle.'

The young man knew there must be something special about the hair but he took it and pretended to twist it round the bridle. But as he returned to his chair he dropped it in the fire. To his dismay, it gave a loud crack and the Draiglin' Hogney jumped.

'What was that?'

'Just a bit of green wood,' said the young man.

'Maybe,' muttered the Draiglin' Hogney. 'And maybe not. Does your hound bite?'

'Never.'

'You're an impudent fool and deceitful to boot. Put this round his collar.'

So the young man fiddled with the collar and dropped the hair in the fire. It gave the most almighty crack and the Draiglin' Hogney started.

'Green wood,' said the young man. 'What's the hair supposed to do?'

'Never you mind. No doubt you'll say your hawk never rends either, so

I'll spare myself the question. This is for her jesses.'

He passed over a third hair, which the young man again dropped in the fire. It sounded like the crack of doom and the Draiglin' Hogney shot a good foot out of his chair.

'You should see your wood's seasoned better,' said the young man. 'That's the third time that's happened.'

'Well, you'll never hear a fourth because I'm the Draiglin' Hogney and I'm going to put you with your brothers!'

Out came the wand and the young man felt himself freeze. Try as he might, he could not move a muscle. The Draiglin' Hogney advanced, grinning horribly, but even as he did so, the hawk swooped at his head, the hound went for his throat and the horse struck him such a mighty blow he was

knocked unconscious. The wand fell
and the young man was released from
his spell. He pointed the wand in his
turn and at once the Draiglin' Hogney
dissolved into thin air and went wailing
off into outer darkness, never to trouble
mankind again.

'And now,' said the youngest son,
'we must search for my brothers.'

They hunted that palace from top
to bottom. They found whole attics
full of treasure and chests so stuffed
with jewels that the lids wouldn't close.
Three days and three nights it took and
at last the hound sniffed out a little
cellar underground with cobwebs round
the door. There lay the two brothers,
fast asleep, and many more besides.
There must have been a score of young
men, all richly dressed and strongly
armed, and all defeated by the magic
of the Draiglin' Hogney. So the

youngest son awakened them with a touch of the magician's staff and sent them on their way, loaded with wealth.

And as for the brothers themselves, they took as much gold as they could carry and returned to their father's house. And there they lived, rich and happy, for the rest of their lives.

This story is by Dinah Starkey.

The Seven Monsters

In Africa there was once a kingdom. In the kingdom, there was a city. In the city was a palace and in the palace lived a king.

He was known as the Oba. He sat on a throne supported by two magnificent bronze leopards and carried a sword shaped like a leaf, covered in the most beautiful patterns, for the King had the best metalsmiths in all Africa. He also had the most careless daughter in all Africa. She cared nothing for her father's greatness and was always to be found running wild in the fields outside the strong, mud walls of the city, laughing and chattering with her six special friends. Never did they think that one day they would be in great danger.

All seven were walking along the path which led through the forest and down to the wide, marshy river. First, however, they had to pass the rocks and, in a cave among the rocks, were seven ugly monsters and they heard the chattering.

'Our dinner walks towards us,' said one monster. 'One for each of us.' He was called Monster Slobber. You can guess why.

'But which of us will eat the King's daughter?' asked Monster Yellow Belly.

'Me,' shouted Monster Snaggle Tooth but so did Monster Short Shanks, and Monster Goggle Eyes and

Monster Dish Face and Monster Blue Nose. 'Me! Me! Me!' and they began to quarrel. Their roars echoed round the cave and the girls heard them. They began to run.

'Run into the forest,' shouted the King's daughter.

'After them,' bellowed the monsters. 'Catch them and eat them!'

The girls ran and the monsters ran but the monsters were bigger and stronger and they ran faster.

'We must climb a tree,' gasped the King's daughter.

The monkeys screamed and swung away as the girls scrambled into the highest branches of a tall tree and clung there, trembling like leaves in the wind.

But the monsters could climb, too, and so they did. Then, CRACK!

They were too heavy. The branches

broke away and they fell to the ground. They stood under the tree and howled. The girls clung to the branches and trembled.

'We must cut the tree down,' said Slobber.

'Go home and fetch an axe,' said Yellow Belly to Snaggle Tooth.

'Why me?' complained Snaggle Tooth. 'The girls might fall out of the tree while I am away and then *you* will eat the King's daughter. Send Short Shanks.'

'Not me,' said Short Shanks. 'You go, Goggle Eyes.'

'I'm not going,' said Goggle Eyes. 'Send Dish Face.'

'Me?' said Dish Face. 'You go, Blue Nose.'

'No,' said Blue Nose and they all stood at the foot of the tree arguing and shouting, 'No, no, no!'

'Then,' said Slobber, 'we must all go together,' and off they hurried to fetch the axe.

As soon as they were out of sight, the girls took off their brightly coloured dresses, hung them in the branches and scrambled down to the ground.

'We must run to Father Rock,' said the King's daughter, 'and ask for help.'

They ran and they ran until they reached a great rock. 'Father Rock,' cried the King's daughter, 'be our father and mother and give us shelter.'

The rock opened slowly and the girls crept into the cool of its dark centre. Then the rock closed itself again and the girls were hidden.

By that time, the monsters had returned to the tree. They were hot, for the sun was high. They looked up at the bright dresses, fluttering in the

breeze and said, 'Soon we shall have them. What a feast!' and licked their lips.

Chop, chop, chop! Soon the tree was swaying, the tree was groaning and then it fell with a mighty crash.

'What is this?' said Slobber, tearing at the dresses with his big claws. 'These are just clothes.' He bellowed angrily, 'They have tricked us!'

Goggle Eyes looked carefully at the ground. 'See these footprints in the sand? They went this way. Follow the footprints.' And they set off after the girls, pounding along.

Soon, the footprints stopped, right in front of a great rock.

'They are inside the rock,' muttered Slobber. 'Open, Rock,' he ordered.

'I will not,' replied the rock.

'Then the rock must be split open,' declared Slobber.

'Go home and fetch a hammer,' said Yellow Belly to Snaggle Tooth.

'Why me?' complained Snaggle Tooth. 'The girls might come out before I get back then *you* will eat the King's daughter. Send Short Shanks.'

'Not me,' said Short Shanks. 'You go, Goggle Eyes.'

'I'm not going,' said Goggle Eyes. 'Send Dish Face.'

'Me?' said Dish Face. 'You go, Blue Nose.'

'No,' said Blue Nose and they all stood in front of the rock, arguing and shouting, 'No, no, no!'

'Then,' said Slobber, 'it seems that we must all go together,' and they ran home to fetch the hammer, puffing and grumbling in the heat of the sun.

As soon as they had gone, the rock spoke. 'Come out now and run for your lives,' and he opened up and the girls ran out and down the path towards the big, wide river.

The monsters came back to the rock and swung the big hammer.

'It's no use hammering me,' the rock told them. 'They've gone.'

The monsters howled with rage and flung the hammer at the rock. Now they were very hot and very angry but in the distance they could see the girls running across the open plain and set off after them.

The girls ran on but they had left the trees and rocks behind. They were running down through the marshes. As they ran, a flock of brilliant birds rose from the water, calling anxiously. Where could they hide? The King's daughter looked back and saw the monsters coming closer and closer.

'Run into the reeds,' she panted. 'We must ask Father Toad for help.'

Father Toad sat in the reed bed and watched the girls.

'Father Toad,' cried the King's daughter, 'be our father and mother. Hide us from the monsters.'

'You will be a big mouthful,' croaked Father Toad, 'but I will do my best,' and he began to puff himself up. He swelled and swelled. He grew bigger and bigger until the girls could creep in his mouth and rest safely inside him.

In no time, the monsters were there.

'Father Toad,' they roared, 'the girls are ours. Spit them out or it will be the worse for you.'

'All right,' said Father Toad. 'Don't make a fuss. Line up and I'll spit them out.'

But Father Toad was filling his cheeks with lead bullets which he often found lying in the marsh and kept in his storehouse under the reeds. When the monsters were in a line, he began to spit out the bullets.

First, Monster Slobber fell, then Yellow Belly.

'Spit out the King's daughter,' shouted the other monsters.

'Very well,' said Father Toad, 'come closer.' But he spat out one, two, three more bullets and Snaggle Tooth, Short Shanks and Goggle Eyes fell dead, too.

'We said the King's daughter,' yelled Dish Face and Blue Nose, for monsters care only for themselves.

'I'm getting there,' replied Father Toad but one, two and Dish Face and Blue Nose were lying dead on the ground.

Then Father Toad hopped out of the reed bed and made his way to the King's well. He sat there until the women came to fetch water, balancing their pots on their heads.

'Take this message to the King,' said Father Toad. 'Tell him to spread his best woven carpet between his palace and this well.'

When the King had done as he had been asked, Father Toad spat out one: the King's daughter and then: two, three, four, five, six little friends and they ran crying and laughing to tell the King of their adventure.

Then the King gave a great feast, a celebration with drums, at which the King's daughter and her friends danced their adventure with the monsters. But the King knew who he must thank and had cakes and sweet things carried to Father Toad. He also asked his best metalsmiths to make a little golden crown for Father Toad which he wears to this day down in the reed bed.

This retelling of a story from Africa is by Pat Thomson.

The Dragon on the Roof

A long time ago in a remote part of
China, a dragon once flew down from
the mountains and settled on the roof
of the house of a rich merchant.

The merchant and his wife and
family and servants were, of course,
terrified out of their wits. They looked
out of the windows and could see the
shadows of the dragon's wings
stretching out over the ground below
them. And when they looked up, they
could see his great yellow claws
sticking into the roof above them.

'What are we going to do?' cried the merchant's wife.

'Perhaps it'll be gone in the morning,' said the merchant. 'Let's go to bed and hope.'

So they all went to bed and lay there shivering and shaking. And nobody slept a wink all night. They just lay there listening to the sound of the dragon's leathery wings beating on the walls behind their beds, and the scraping of the dragon's scaly belly on the tiles above their heads.

The next day, the dragon was still there, warming its tail on the chimney pot. And no-one in the house dared to stick so much as a finger out of doors.

'We can't go on like this!' cried the merchant's wife. 'Sometimes dragons stay like that for a thousand years!'

So once again they waited until

nightfall, but this time the merchant and his family and servants crept out of the house as quiet as could be. They could hear the dragon snoring away high above them, and they could feel the warm breeze of his breath blowing down their necks, as they tiptoed across the lawns. By the time they got halfway across, they were so frightened that they all suddenly started to run. They ran out of the gardens and off into the night. And they didn't stop running until they'd reached the great city, where the king of that part of China lived.

The next day, the merchant went to the King's palace. Outside the gates was a huge crowd of beggars and poor people and ragged children, and the rich merchant had to fight his way through them.

'What do you want?' demanded

the palace guard.

'I want to see the King,' exclaimed the merchant.

'Buzz off!' said the guard.

'I don't want charity!' replied the merchant. 'I'm a rich man!'

'Oh, then in you go!' said the guard.

So the merchant entered the palace, and found the King playing Fiddlesticks with his Lord High Chancellor in the Council Chamber. The merchant fell on his face in front of the King, and cried, 'O Great King! Favourite of His People! Help me! The Jade Dragon has flown down from the Jade Dragon Snow Mountain, and has alighted on my rooftop, O Most Beloved Ruler Of All China!'

The King (who was, in fact, extremely unpopular) paused for a moment in his game and looked at the merchant, and said, 'I don't particularly like your hat.'

So the merchant, of course, threw his hat out of the window, and said, 'O Monarch Esteemed By All His Subjects! Loved By All The World! Please assist me and my wretched family! The Jade Dragon has flown down from the Jade Dragon Snow Mountain, and is, at this very moment, sitting on my rooftop, and refuses to go away!'

The King turned again, and glared at the merchant, and said, 'Nor do I much care for your trousers.'

So the merchant, naturally, removed his trousers and threw them out of the window.

'Nor,' said the King, 'do I really approve of anything you are wearing.'

So, of course, the merchant took off all the rest of his clothes, and stood there stark naked in front of the King, feeling very embarrassed.

'*And* throw them out of the window!' said the King.

So the merchant threw them out of the window. At which point the King burst out into the most unpleasant laughter. 'It must be your birthday,' he cried, 'because you're wearing your birthday suit!' And he collapsed on the floor helpless with mirth. (You can see why he wasn't a very popular king.)

Finally, however, the King pulled himself together and asked, 'Well, what do you want? You can't stand around here stark naked, you know!'

'Your Majesty!' cried the merchant. 'The Jade Dragon has flown down from the Jade Dragon Snow Mountain and is sitting on my rooftop!'

The King went a little green about the gills when he heard this, because nobody particularly likes having a dragon in their kingdom.

'Well, what do you expect me to do about it?' replied the King. 'Go and read it a bedtime story?'

'Oh no! Most Cherished Lord! Admired and Venerated Leader of His People! No-one would expect *you* to read bedtime stories to a dragon. But I was hoping you might find some way of . . . getting rid of it?'

'Is it a big dragon?' asked the King.

'It is. Very big,' replied the merchant.

'I was afraid it would be,' said the King. 'And have you tried asking it – politely – if it would mind leaving of its own accord?'

'First thing we did,' said the merchant.

'Well, in that case,' replied the King, '. . . tough luck!'

Just at that moment there was a terrible noise from outside the palace.

'Ah! It's here!' cried the King, leaping onto a chair. 'The dragon's come to get us!'

'No, no, no,' said the Lord High Chancellor. 'That is nothing to be worried about. It is merely the poor people of your kingdom groaning at your gates, because they have not enough to eat.'

'Miserable wretches!' cried the King. 'Have them all beaten and sent home.'

'Er . . . many of them have no homes to go to,' replied the Chancellor.

'Well then – obviously – just have them beaten!' exclaimed the King. 'And sent somewhere else to groan.'

But just then there was an even louder roar from outside the palace gates.

'*That*'s the dragon!' exclaimed the King, hiding in a cupboard.

'No,' said the Chancellor, 'that is

merely the rest of your subjects demanding that you resign the crown.'

At this point, the King sat on his throne and burst into tears. 'Why does nobody like me?' he cried.

'Er . . . may I go and put some clothes on?' asked the merchant.

'Oh! Go and jump out of the window!' replied the King.

Well, the merchant was just going to jump out of the window (because, of course, in those days, whenever a king told you to do something, you always did it) when the Lord High Chancellor stopped him and turned to the King and whispered, 'Your Majesty! It may be that this fellow's dragon could be just what we need!'

'Don't talk piffle,' snapped the King. '*Nobody* needs a dragon!'

'On the contrary,' replied the Chancellor, '*you* need one right now.

Nothing, you know, makes a king more popular with his people than getting rid of a dragon for them.'

'You're right!' exclaimed the King.

So there and then he sent for the Most Famous Dragon-Slayer In The Land, and had it announced that a terrible dragon had flown down from the Jade Dragon Snow Mountain and was threatening their kingdom.

Naturally everyone immediately forgot about being hungry or discontented. They fled from the palace gates and hid themselves away in dark corners for fear of the dragon.

Some days later, the Most Famous Dragon-Slayer In The Whole Of China arrived. The King ordered a fabulous banquet in his honour. But the Dragon-Slayer said, 'I never eat so much as a nut, nor drink so much as a

thimbleful, until I have seen my
dragon, and know what it is I have to
do.'

So the merchant took the Dragon-
Slayer to his house, and they hid in an
apricot tree to observe the dragon.

'Well? What d'you think of it?' asked
the merchant.

But the Dragon-Slayer said not a
word.

'Big, isn't it?' said the merchant.

But the Dragon-Slayer remained
silent. He just sat there in the apricot
tree, watching the dragon.

'How are you going to kill it?'
enquired the merchant eagerly.

But the Dragon-Slayer didn't reply.
He climbed down out of the apricot
tree, and returned to the palace. There
he ordered a plate of eels and mint,
and he drank a cup of wine.

When he had finished, the King

looked at him anxiously and said,
'Well? What are you going to do?'

The Dragon-Slayer wiped his mouth
and said, 'Nothing.'

'Nothing?' exclaimed the King. 'Is
this dragon so big you're frightened of
it?'

'I've killed bigger ones,' replied the
Dragon-Slayer, rubbing his chest.

'Is it such a fierce dragon you're
scared it'll finish you off?' cried the
King.

'I've dispatched hundreds of fiercer
ones,' yawned the Dragon-Slayer.

'Then has it hotter breath?'
demanded the King. 'Or sharper claws?
Or bigger jaws? Or what?'

But the Dragon-Slayer merely shut
his eyes and said, 'Like me, it's old and
tired. It has come down from the
mountains to die in the East. It's merely
resting on that rooftop. It'll do no

harm, and, in a week or so, it will go on its way to the place where dragons go to die.'

Then the Dragon-Slayer rolled himself up in his cloak and went to sleep by the fire.

But the King was furious.

'This is no good!' he whispered to the Lord High Chancellor. 'It's not going to make me more popular if I leave this dragon sitting on that man's rooftop. It needs to be killed!'

'I agree,' replied the Lord High Chancellor. 'There's nothing like a little dragon-slaying to get the people on to your side.'

So the King sent for the Second Most Famous Dragon-Slayer In The Whole Of China, and said, 'Listen! I want you to kill that dragon, and I won't pay you unless you do!'

So the Second Most Famous

Dragon-Slayer In The Whole Of China went to the merchant's house and hid in the apricot tree to observe the dragon. Then he came back to the palace, and ordered a plate of pork and beans, drank a flask of wine, and said to the King, 'It's a messy business killing dragons. The fire from their nostrils burns the countryside, and their blood poisons the land so that nothing will grow for a hundred years. And when you cut them open, the smoke from their bellies covers the sky and blots out the sun.'

But the King said, 'I want that dragon killed. Mess or no mess!'

But the Second Most Famous Dragon-Slayer In The Of China replied, 'Best to leave this one alone. It's old and on its way to die in the East.'

Whereupon the King stamped his

foot, and sent for the Third Most Famous Dragon-Slayer In The Whole Of China, and said, 'Kill me that dragon!'

Now the Third Most Famous Dragon-Slayer In The Whole Of China also happened to be the most cunning, and he knew just why it was the King was so keen to have the dragon killed. He also knew that if he killed the dragon, he himself would become the First Dragon-Slayer In The Whole Of China instead of only the Third. So he said to the King, 'Nothing easier, Your Majesty. I'll kill that dragon straightaway.'

Well, he went to the merchant's house, climbed the apricot tree and looked down at the dragon. He could see it was an old one and weary of life, and he congratulated himself on his good luck. But he told the King to have it announced in the market square that the dragon was young and fierce and very dangerous, and that everyone should keep well out of the way until after the battle was over.

When they heard this, of course, the people were even more frightened, and they hurried back to their hiding places and shut their windows and bolted their doors.

Then the Dragon-Slayer shouted down from the apricot tree, 'Wake up, Jade Dragon! For I have come to kill you!'

The Jade Dragon opened a weary eye and said, 'Leave me alone, Dragon-Slayer. I am old and weary of life. I have come down from the Jade Dragon Snow Mountain to die in the East. Why should you kill me?'

'Enough!' cried the Dragon-Slayer. 'If you do not want me to kill you, fly away and never come back.'

The Jade Dragon opened its other weary eye and looked at the Dragon-Slayer. 'Dragon-Slayer! You know I am too weary to fly any further. I have settled here to rest. I shall do no-one any harm. Let me be.'

But the Dragon-Slayer didn't reply. He took his bow and he took two arrows, and he let one arrow fly, and it pierced the Jade Dragon in the right eye. The old creature roared in pain, and tried to raise itself up on its legs, but it was too old and weak, and it fell down again on top of the house, crushing one of the walls beneath its weight.

Then the Dragon-Slayer fired his second arrow, and it pierced the Jade Dragon in the left eye, and the old

creature roared again and a sheet of
fire shot out from its nostrils and set
fire to the apricot tree.

But the Dragon-Slayer had leapt out
of the tree and onto the back of the
blinded beast, as it struggled to its feet,
breathing flames through its nostrils
and setting fire to the countryside all
around.

It flapped its old, leathery wings,
trying to fly away, but the Dragon-
Slayer was hanging onto the spines on
its back, and he drove his long sword
deep into the dragon's side. And the
Jade Dragon howled, and its claws
ripped off the roof of the merchant's
house, as it rolled over on its side and
its blood gushed out onto the ground.

And everywhere the dragon's blood
touched the earth, the plants turned
black and withered away.

Then the Dragon-Slayer took his

long sword and cut open the old dragon's fiery belly, and a black cloud shot up into the sky and covered the sun.

When the people looked out of their hiding places, they thought the night had fallen, the sky was so black. All around the city they could see the countryside burning, and the air stank with the smell of the dragon's blood. But the King ordered a great banquet to be held in the palace that night, and he paid the Dragon-Slayer half the money he had in his treasury.

And when the people heard that the dragon had been killed, they cheered and clapped and praised the King because he had saved them from the dragon.

When the merchant and his wife and children returned to their house, however, they found it was just a pile of rubble, and their beautiful lawns and gardens were burnt beyond repair.

And the sun did not shine again in that land all that summer, because of the smoke from the dragon's belly. What is worse, nothing would grow in that kingdom for a hundred years, because the land had been poisoned by the dragon's blood.

But the odd thing is, that although the people were now poorer than they ever had been, and scarcely ever had enough to eat or saw the sun, every time the King went out they cheered him and clapped him and called him 'King Chong The Dragon-Slayer', and he was, from that time on, the most popular ruler in the whole of China for as long as he reigned and long after.

And the Third Most Famous Dragon-Slayer In The Whole Of

China became the First, and people never tired of telling and retelling the story of his fearful fight with the Jade Dragon from the Jade Dragon Snow Mountain.

What do you think of that?

This story is by Terry Jones.

Finn mac Cumaill

Finn mac Cumaill – sometimes called
Fingal – was the son of Cumaill, leader
of the Fianna, or the Fenians, as they
were also called. They were a
legendary band of warriors whose
amazing exploits are the subject of
many stories told in both Ireland and
Scotland.

When Cumaill, the chief of the Fianna,
was killed in battle by his rival, his wife
feared for her life, and fled to the
woods. There she had a son, Finn, and

to keep him out of the clutches of
Cumaill's enemies she left him in the
care of two women. One was a druid,
Bobdall, and the other, Fiacal, was a
warrior.

By the time he was six Finn was as
strong as a young man, and possessed
the skills of a hero. The two women
taught him to run by chasing him day
after day through the woods with a
stick, until he was quicker than smoke
in the wind. They taught him to swim
by throwing him into the river, again
and again, until his body slipped
through the water as easily as the
shadow of a cloud.

But in time, Finn mac Cumaill,
wanting to see something of the world,
ran away from his stern teachers. He
lived first amongst poets and learned
by heart long poems with great wisdom
in them. Then he worked for a year in

the forge of a smith, and made a sword for himself. Finally he decided it was time for him to journey to the sacred city of Tara, the home of the Fianna. He arrived in time for the feast of Samain, the time when summer ends and winter begins the new year. At this season, the doors of the Siodh are opened and there are no barriers between the world of light and the underworld.

All kings and chiefs were welcome to feast at Tara during Samain, but the young Finn was not yet a king or chief, and he was also a stranger. But his bearing was that of a hero, and as soon as he said, 'I am Finn, son of Cumaill,' he was able to enter the great hall and eat and drink with the rest. He watched kings deep in talk, servants going to and fro with gold dishes and jugs, dogs wrestling for bones. He gazed at beautiful women, and the quick hands of harp players. And yet this feast seemed to be too quiet for a celebration, a feast without real joy. He noticed that as the evening wore on the talk grew quieter, the music sadder.

The Chain of Silence was shaken and the talk and music stopped completely. Conn, the High King of Tara, spoke: 'Fellow kings and friends, you know that tonight Aillen will come again. In a few hours, unless we prevent it, these walls and timbers will blacken in the searing flames he carries. Some of us will die. Which of us will then prevent it? Who will preserve Tara against Aillen, the Wraith of Fire?'

There was no need to shake the Chain of Silence again. None of the heroes spoke. One stared into his wine as if his courage were drowned there, another pulled at his beard, another drew his finger round the rim of a cup.

Until he heard Conn's words, Finn did not know of the terrible thing that had taken place every Samain for nine years past. Aillen mac Midna, grandson of the lord of the underworld, emerged from the dark below the world to attack the holy city of Tara. Each year he attacked with flame, but first Aillen sent harp music as soothing and quietly beautiful as the murmur of lake waters in summer. The music swirled over the land, lulling all the listeners into deep sleep, then Aillen hurled fearsome blue fire into the city and broke its walls, causing terror and death. Each year Tara had been rebuilt but now, again, the city awaited Samain with dread.

That was what caused so shameful a moment of hesitation. It was ended when Finn stood up. 'I am Finn, son of Cumaill. I will face the music and then the fire of Aillen, provided that due reward comes to me after my victory.'

A hundred stupefied faces gazed at Finn.

'All that I can give I will give,' said Conn.

It was enough for Finn. Out he strode into the dark, past the flickering torches, over rampart after rampart, till he stood under the stars. Fingers resting on his sword-handle, he listened to the noises of the night, straining for a hint of the wraith's approach. The night was totally still, but Finn's hearing, trained for years on the smallest scraps of sound, made out the restless shifting of reeds at the lake's edge, the scurry of a rat across mud, the stab of a heron's beak. From the silence round these few sounds he knew that the wraith had still to make its first move.

'Finn mac Cumaill!' a voice whispered behind him from the dark. Finn whisked round, but the figure emerging from the dark was an old warrior who spoke as a friend.

'Many years ago your father saved my life. This spear will save yours.' The spear that the old warrior offered Finn was wrapped in a sack.

'Why is it covered?' Finn asked.

'It is dangerous. Uncovered, it aches to fly like a hawk from the hand. This famished steel pursues its prey with the hunger of a falcon after a long fast.'

'What is its name?'

'Its name is Birga. It was forged by Lein, the smith of the gods. He beat the fire of the sun into it, and the power of the moon. Its head is hammered to the

shaft with thirty rivets of Arabian gold.
Your father took it from Aillen. It is
Aillen's own spear that waits to find
him out. But do nothing until the
music steals across the dark plain like
mist. Then press the cold steel against
your cheek. You will not sleep then.
Soon the music will fade, and Aillen
will make ready to hurl his breath of
blue fire. At the first sight of flame you
must take aim. Then be ready to
gather the flame in your cloak, and
release Birga.'

'And there is nothing else?'

'Only one thing. Be prepared, when
you uncover Birga, for your head to
swim. Birga has been hurled into a
hundred horrors and the stench of the
past hangs round it. And now I must
go. I dare not hear one note of the
harp of Aillen.'

With that the old warrior turned and

went. Finn heard his footsteps fade,
then he faced the dark again.

He did not have long to wait. Ten
times softer than a faint whisper in the
reeds came the first tremble of harp
strings. A single note grew and spread
till it was a mist of shimmering sound.
It was as if, from the dark in front of
him, every reed and grass blade, every
creature and every pool of quiet water
poured its own murmuring earth-music
through the strings of Aillen's appalling
harp.

Finn felt himself listening, hung
round with chains of sound. He felt
himself tranced and tipping over to
sleep. With a surge of panic he
uncovered Birga and clasped the
blade to his cheek. There was an
overwhelming smell of decay that
made him feel sick, then his head
cleared and the spear quivered in

his hand like a living thing.

A thin strand of moon glimmered in front of him and faded. Then another. And another. Finn realized that he was looking at moonlit harp strings and that the drifting mists were Aillen's cloudy, white hands moving over the strings.

Nearer and nearer the wraith came. Finn could now see the outline of the whole body. He could make out a great head, pale as a slug's, a dark well of a mouth. As he watched, the dark red jaws pulled open wider and from them poured a torrent of greeny-blue, crackling light. It came surging towards Finn, writhing and leaping like a mountain stream in flood. Finn pointed his spear at the hissing light and spread his cloak wide. The flames found the tip of the spear, and a fierce, blue-white light roared and foamed

along it, shaking Finn's whole body, then writhed down into the folds of his cloak. Dying flames ran here and there, merging into each other, and went out. Only a few thin shreds of fire fell to the ground, flickered and died.

Finn hurled Birga. It screamed from his hand towards Aillen, who was already hurrying back in a trembling fuzz of grey light towards the entrance to his underworld. Birga reached Aillen before Aillen reached safety. The last thing Aillen saw was the welcome green light of the underworld filtering from the opening doorway. Then the green light faded.

Aillen had made his last raid on Tara. Finn found his body and hacked off the head as proof of what he had accomplished, then set off through the dawn to claim his reward from Conn the High King.

And so it was that Finn mac Cumaill gained the leadership of the Fianna.

This story is by Robert Hull.

Julie Parker's Enormous Secret

'I've got a puppy called Boxo. He chews slippers and eats newspapers,' said Jeremy Price.

'I've got a rabbit. He burrows into next door's garden,' said Jamie Smart. 'He's called Digger.'

Class 1 were talking about pets. Julie Parker hadn't really got a pet — well, not a real one — only the spider who lived on the ceiling in her bedroom. She'd named him Spinner after he'd spun a droopy thread across to the window. Julie put up her hand to tell them about Spinner, then took it down again. They might laugh at her. It wasn't fair. She was the only person in the class without a proper pet.

'I know someone who's got a horse,' said Sally Pontin, stroking her plait then putting the end of it in her mouth. Julie looked out of the window.

'I know someone who has an elephant,' said Paul King, and there was a big cheeky grin on his face.

'Don't tell me,' said Miss Boswell. 'Someone knows someone who has a dinosaur! Now enough is enough, Class 1. It's playtime. Out you all go.'

But enough was not enough for Julie Parker. She'd just remembered some-thing the caretaker had said. She went to join Sally Pontin and Mary Moss, who were playing hairdressers. Mary had just arranged Sally's plait on top of her head to make her look grown-up.

'Shall I tell you a secret?' Julie said to them, then, before they could say no, went on, 'I know where there is an *enormous* pet. It belongs to the caretaker.'

'Where?' said Mary.

'It's locked up behind the old blue door at the back of the school.'

'How do you know?' said Sally, moving all Mary's slides together so they looked like fighting insects.

'He told me.'

'What is it, then?' asked Mary.

'Well, it's a secret really, but I'll tell you. It's . . .'

'Brrm brrm brrm.' Paul King zoomed into them, his arms held wide. He was making a dreadful screeching noise.

'Go away,' said Julie angrily.

'Yes, stop it,' said Mary, who didn't like loud noises. 'Julie's going to tell us a secret.'

'Good, I'll stay,' said Paul King. Julie looked round the playground, then in a hushed voice said, 'It lives behind that old . . .'

Crash, bang. Jamie Smart, Jeremy Price and a crushed Coke can sort of fell into them. Jamie Smart stood up, rubbing his knee. Julie took no notice of Jeremy Price. She took no notice of the Coke can. She was feeling excited, was Julie Parker, and her cheeks were getting warm.

'It's a *dragon*.'

'What!' said Jamie Smart. He stopped rubbing his knee and gave a huge silly laugh.

'What!' shouted Paul King. 'A dragon? Don't believe you.'

'What, never!' said Jeremy Price. He kicked an apple core over the school roof and whistled at his own cleverness.

'All right, follow me.' Jeremy Price

went silent. Sally Pontin moved Mary's slides back into a friendly position, and Mary Moss put her thumb in her mouth. 'That's if you're not too scared,' said Julie.

She took Mary's hand. 'Come on,' she said, 'you'll be all right with me. She can't get out.'

'She!' said Jeremy Price.

'Yes,' said Julie, 'the dragon's a she.' Julie set off down the passageway to the back of the school. Jamie Smart and Jeremy Price pushed into her, but Julie wouldn't be hurried. She stopped in front of the old blue door. It had a black bar across the middle and grilles on the top half.

'There now,' she said. 'Put your hand near the grilles.' No-one moved. They just shuffled. Then Jeremy Price dared Jamie Smart to have a go. Jamie reached up.

'It's hot,' he said.

'Yes,' said Julie, 'that's the dragon's breath. Sometimes it steams.'

'Oh, go on,' said Jeremy Price. He was the tallest boy in the class. He was also the biggest show-off. He reached up to the grilles and poked three fingers through.

'I'm not scared,' he said. But suddenly there was a dreadful roaring noise from inside, and a gush of hot air made the blue wooden door judder. Mary screamed. Jamie Smart wailed like a siren and Jeremy Price pulled his fingers out. He rushed back down the passageway and leaned against the wall, nursing his three fingers. He had a very white face, had Jeremy Price.

'Quick,' said Julie Parker. 'Miss Boswell's coming,' but nobody moved.

'Did I see you playing in the passageway, Class 1?' said Miss Boswell.

'Only the caretaker's allowed down there. You should know that.' She gave Jeremy Price her coffee-cup to take back to the staff room. It rattled on the saucer. Jeremy Price was still shaking.

Julie Parker couldn't settle after playtime. She squirmed on her chair, then sat with one leg doubled underneath her and gazed out of the window. Miss Boswell walked round the classroom, watering the plants. She liked watering plants, did Miss Boswell.

'Please . . .' began Jeremy Price.

'Yes?' Miss Boswell poked a finger into the soil of the Busy Lizzie plant.

'Does the caretaker really have a dragon behind that blue door?'

Miss Boswell removed her finger from the pot and stood still for a second, then titter-toed back to the desk. She was wearing her highest heels.

'I must say, Class 1, I didn't know there was a dragon behind the blue door.'

'There is, there is,' said Jamie Smart. 'Julie told us. We heard it roar.'

'Well, fancy,' said Miss Boswell. 'Did it breathe fire?'

Julie Parker unhooked her leg and fell off her chair.

'No need to get excited, Julie,' said Miss Boswell. 'I'm sure the caretaker can handle the dragon. Now enough is enough, Class 1.' Class 1 usually stopped chattering when Miss Boswell said those words, but today they didn't.

'It nearly ate Jeremy's fingers,' said Mary Moss, who rarely said anything out loud. Julie poked Mary in the back with a ruler. Jeremy Price poked her in the side with his pencil.

'Shut up,' he said, but it was too late.

'Jeremy put his fingers through the

grille,' Mary was saying.

Miss Boswell looked cross. 'That was a very silly thing to do, Jeremy Price. You might have been burned. Don't ever do it again.' Jeremy bit his lip and frowned.

Miss Boswell put some sums on the board, then settled down to a good search in her handbag. She didn't see Mr Binns, the caretaker, open the classroom door. He stood there in his blue overalls and flat cap with the feather.

'Can I borrow Julie Parker for a moment?' he said. 'I'd like a word with her.' Miss Boswell jumped. The class went quiet. Julie gripped the sides of her chair. Mr Binns beckoned to her with his podgy finger. Slowly Julie got up and went to the door. She followed him down the corridor and out of the building. Mr Binns said nothing. He just whistled. They went down the passageway and stopped in front of the blue door.

'There's a surprise in there for you, my girl. It's a bit hot inside. Mind how you go.' Julie bit her lip. She turned to look behind.

Miss Boswell and the whole of Class 1 were thundering towards them.

'Wait for us,' shouted Miss Boswell. 'You might need our help.'

'We want to see the dragon,' said Jeremy Price. 'Wait for us.' They crowded behind Julie. Sally Pontin was standing very near Miss Boswell. She looked scared.

'Go on, Julie,' said Jamie Smart.

'Be careful,' said Mary Moss in a weak voice. Julie tiptoed inside. The heat made her feel dizzy, and then the door slammed shut. She was alone in a hot dim room covered in cobwebs. She

thought of Spinner. He liked webs.
However, the door opened again and
Mr Binns stepped in. A low rumbling
was coming from the corner. Julie
started sweating. Then suddenly
through the dimness she heard a voice.

'Miaow,' it said, 'miaow.'

'Over here,' said Mr Binns. 'Come
on, Julie. Don't touch anything.' In the
corner next to a large pipe was a
cardboard box. Inside, three small grey
kittens snuggled against a huge mother
cat.

'There,' said Mr Binns proudly.
'Their eyes have just opened, and guess
what? Your mother tells me you haven't
got a pet. She also tells me you can
have one of these. How about that?'

'Oh,' said Julie. Her eyes prickled in
the dry heat. 'Oh, thank you,' she said,
then, because she couldn't think what
else to say, she said three more 'ohs'.

Mr Binns carried the kitten to the door for the rest of Class 1 to see, and everyone, including Miss Boswell, said, 'Oh' – until suddenly they were stopped by an enormous roar from behind the blue door. Mary Moss grabbed Miss Boswell's skirt.

Mr Binns turned towards the doorway. 'Stop it,' he yelled. He turned back to Class 1. 'That's the boiler,' he said. 'Roars like a bloomin' dragon, she does. Fair scares you when she steams up.' Class 1 burst out laughing, and Mr Binns, who didn't know what was funny, pushed up his cap with the feather and scratched his head. He leaned forward and gently stroked the kitten's fur with just one finger.

'What are you going to call your kitten, Julie?' he said.

'How about Dragon?' said Jeremy Price, and he gave Julie's arm a neat pinch just above the elbow.

Julie, with rather pink cheeks and a funny sort of smile, said that Dragon was not a very good name for a cat, but what about Smoky. Would that do? Jeremy Price grinned wickedly and said it would, and the rest of Class 1 agreed. Yes, Smoky sounded just about right for a dragon who turned out to be a kitten.

This story is by Margaret Nash.

Perseus and Andromeda

The land of Ethiopia was once ruled by
a king and queen called Cepheus and
Cassiopeia; and they had an only
daughter, Andromeda. One day the
queen was foolish enough to boast that
her daughter was more lovely than the
Nereids – the lovely sea nymphs
protected by the sea god Poseidon.

Beautiful as she was, the princess
could not compare with the Nereids;
and Poseidon would not forgive the
queen for her idle boast.

As punishment he sent a huge sea

serpent, Cetus, to devour anyone who ventured out to sea. So the fishermen could not sail their boats and starvation threatened the land.

When King Cepheus consulted his wise men, they told him, 'The only way to calm Poseidon's fury is to sacrifice what you love best.'

It did not take the king long to realize what that meant.

'I love my daughter most of all,' he sadly said.

There clearly was no choice. In great sorrow, the king and queen had to watch as their daughter was chained to a rock not far from shore.

At around that time, the young god Perseus, son of Zeus, father of the gods, was flying over Egypt eastwards towards Ethiopia. On his journey he suddenly saw the lovely maiden chained to a rock, her dark hair

streaming in the breeze. Tears flowed down her lovely cheeks as the cruel sea crashed against the ledge on which she lay.

So moved was Perseus by her plight that he flew down to the shore. Andromeda's parents stood, gazing helplessly at the rock. No-one surely could save their daughter from the serpent's jaws.

When Perseus heard the story, he vowed, 'I will rescue her and slay the monster. In my pouch I have the head of the hideous snake-woman Medusa; it can turn anyone to stone merely by looking at them. And when I'm done, I'll take your daughter as my wife.'

The king and queen readily agreed.

'But first you must kill the monster,' said the king.

Right at that moment, frightened shouts echoed along the shore.

'It's coming! The serpent is coming!'

People were pointing to the churning, foaming waves on the horizon. Perseus rose straight into the air, clutching his sharp sword. As the onlookers stood in awe, he hovered over Andromeda's rock, awaiting the great sea beast.

In a few moments, they could clearly see the beast; its huge tail was thrashing the water into snowy foam, the swirling of its coils made great eddies in the sea, and plumes of water hissed from its nostrils. The waves that raced to shore smashed the little fishing boats to pieces.

The evil monster did not notice Perseus approaching from behind, hanging over it like an eagle about to dive on its prey.

All at once, the young god plunged his sword into the flesh just behind the serpent's scaly head. Cetus reared up, stung by the blow, and lashed at Perseus with its tail. But the god rose high in the air, just in time to avoid its deadly sting.

Again and again he struck at the serpent until the dark blue sea had turned to crimson foam from the serpent's blood. At last, with a groaning and hissing, the monster rose from the water, then sank back, vanishing for ever into the seething sea.

All the onlookers gave a great shout of joy. The king and queen were overcome with happiness: their daughter was saved. Alighting on the rock to unchain Andromeda, Perseus then bore her to the shore.

'I've kept my word and slain the serpent,' he cried. 'Now I claim my bride.'

Andromeda's parents arranged the

wedding without delay. There was good cause for haste. For just as the guests were toasting the health of the happy pair, the doors of the palace burst open. And in rushed a great band of men armed with spears and swords.

It was the army of Prince Phineus.

'Andromeda is promised to me!' Phineus cried. 'I come to claim her.'

'Is this true?' asked Perseus, turning to the king.

'Sadly it is,' the king replied, red with shame. 'My daughter was promised to this man.'

Turning to Phineus, the king said sternly, 'But you forfeited that right when you left my daughter to her fate. She now belongs to Perseus.'

'Then he shall die!' cried Phineus.

It was an uneven battle. Since Phineus's army far outnumbered the king's men, the fight soon began to go against them. Suddenly, Perseus leapt upon a table and called out for all to hear, 'Let all who are my friends turn their gaze away!'

So saying, he pulled Medusa's head from his goatskin pouch and held it in the air. It truly was a terrible sight: a woman's face with black staring eyes and writhing snakes for hair.

'Your trickery does not deceive us!' shouted Phineus.

'Then look closely,' said Perseus, 'and you shall forever be a stone image of a coward.'

Perseus forced him to look full into Medusa's eyes.

Instantly, Phineus became a stone statue aiming a spear.

Perseus had won his bride and soon took her home to Greece.

If you look into the night sky, you may see Perseus, a constellation in the

Milky Way. He is wearing a peaked cap; with one hand he is beckoning to Andromeda, with the other he is rescuing her from the rock. The chain that fastened Andromeda to the rock is dangling from her outstretched arm. Just below her is the mouth of the sea serpent Cetus sent to devour her.

This retelling of a story from Ancient Greece is by James Riordan.

The Liquorice Tree

Old Mrs Abelsea had very regular habits.

'You *got* to have,' she said, 'to get all the work done *and* bring up two grandsons.'

The grandsons were called Mat and Rod. Their mother was a sailor, their father was a merman, in fact the king of the sea. So it was Mrs Abelsea who looked after the boys. Their mother came home at the end of every trip. But sometimes the trips lasted for months and months.

Every morning at seven, Mrs Abelsea got up, went outside, nodded to the morning star, waved to the rooks tumbling round the church tower, and milked the goat. Then she fed the hens and listened to the radio news.

At eight she gave the boys their breakfast: boiled eggs and buttered toast.

'You'll have to keep a look-out today, on the way to school,' she said, one morning. 'On the eight o'clock news, it was. Martians tipped a load of Gondwana beasts all around our village. You better watch out for them.'

'*Gondwana beasts?*'

Both boys stopped eating mid-egg.

'Beasts like they used to have in Gondwana-land, millions of years ago.' Mrs Abelsea pressed her lips together and shook her head. 'The Martians have got them now it seems. And want to get rid of them. Giant snakes, toothy bat-birds, polacanthus, spike-backed tapirs, iguanodons, astrapotheria, mammoths and the like. What *right* do they have to dump their unwanted monsters here? Answer me that!'

Now they could all hear shrill screeches and whistling overhead. There were loud thumps from the village green.

'Finish your eggs first!' said Mrs Abelsea. The boys were wild to get outside. 'And then make your beds, *brush your teeth*, put your homework and packed lunches in your schoolbags – you'll have plenty of time to look at the monsters while you wait for the school bus.'

After she had put away the breakfast dishes, Mrs Abelsea always walked three times barefoot round the village green.

This was to keep up its rating as a piece of common land, where the villagers could pasture their goats and geese. 'Otherwise,' as Mrs Abelsea said, 'some glib-glab is going to build houses over it before you can blow your nose.'

Today, as she walked round the green, Mrs Abelsea noticed an astrapotherium sharpening its snout on the letter box. It was a large hoofed beast of very odd appearance. An aardvark was thoughtfully chewing on a motorbike. A polacanthus, with a row of spikes along its back, was sucking up the contents of a litter bin.

After a few days, the village began to look quite different.

The monsters had heaved the landscape all out of shape. They had scraped some hills quite flat, and had sat down on several houses.

They seemed bored and fretful. And

hungry. Perhaps the diet wasn't quite
what they were used to on Mars.
Pterosauria flew about the sky,
snapping their great toothy jaws,
flapping their wide leathery wings.
Sometimes they snapped up a person.
Ant bears mooched about glumly.
Giant tortoises flattened the hay.
Mammoths chewed the hedges.

Several people went missing.

Mrs Vickers called a village meeting.
She lived next door to Mrs Abelsea, in
a much bigger house, because her
husband was the bank manager.

'There's got to be a rota,' she
announced.

'A rota of *what*?' said Mr Brook, the
postman.

'What's a rota?' asked Mat.

(Mrs Abelsea could not come to the
meeting, so she had told the boys to
go, and listen carefully, and tell her

what was to be done.)

'A rota, a list of people to be eaten by the monsters. In proper order. They eat somebody at least once a week. So – to keep them quiet – we should make up a list. In alphabet order, I suggest. Tie one person to a stake in the middle of the green, say on Saturday. Then the monsters will eat that person, and leave the rest alone. We can start with the names of people who begin with A,' said Mrs Vickers, giving Mat and Rod a nasty look.

Mat and Rod had never got on well with the six Vickers boys, who were called Ben and Len, Ted and Ned, Tom, and Urk. The Vickers boys liked fooling about. This nearly always ended in somebody's car getting smashed. Rod and Mat liked making things. Every now and then, the Vickers boys smashed up the things that Rod and Mat had made.

'But suppose everybody in the village gets eaten?' said Mr Young the parish clerk. 'Then what'll we do?'

'Oh, the Government is sure to have done something by then,' said Mrs Vickers.

Since no-one had a better plan, Mrs Vickers's idea was agreed to.

'We'll start next Saturday,' said Mr Young. 'Anyway, that'll be one less on the school bus.' And he wrote down 'Mat Abelsea'.

The boys went home to tea, and told their grandmother what had been decided.

Now the reason she was not able to come to the meeting was that, every day, exactly at 3.41 in the afternoon, she Listened.

'There is one quiet minute, every day, just at that time,' she had told the boys. 'And if you listen hard, sometimes you get good advice.'

'Who from, Grandma?' the boys asked.

'It's the voice of the Old Ones,' she told them. 'I can hear it; and my old grannie used to hear it; and you boys will hear it by and by, if you grow to be my age.'

But it looked as if the boys never *would* grow to be her age, as their names were first on the list to be eaten by monsters.

Luckily, on this particular afternoon, when she was listening, the Old Ones had spoken to Mrs Abelsea.

'Why not ring up Mars?' they said.

'Ring up Mars, how can we ring up Mars?' Mrs Abelsea grumbled. But Mat and Rod, who were very clever with old bits of wire, and flint, and fibreglass, and sardine tins, saw no problem about that. They made an X-band, solar-beamed, polarized radiophone out of coffee jars, pill bottles, breadcrumbs and the elastic bands the postman dropped on the front doorstep.

Mat rang up Mars and asked for the Controller.

'Mars Head Office here, yes? Can I help you?'

'Look, we are having a lot of trouble from all those monsters you dumped on our village. Can you take them back?'

'So sorry, so sorry,' said the Controller to Mars. He sounded as if he had a mouthful of Martian marbles. That was because of the interstellar translation screen. 'Was a bad mistake to dump them. Due to wrongly spelt office memo. Said *Earth*, should have said *Earda*. Earda is a small moon of Venus where no-one lives. So sorry, will not happen again.'

'But it's happened *now*, and people are being eaten, and all our hills and trees are being heaved about. Will you take the monsters back?'

'So sorry, so sorry. Not possible. Monster-dumping is one-way. No way to reverse. Have a nice day.'

'Well – at least – tell us, how we can get rid of them?' shouted Mat.

'Try sound. Try unnatural sound. Monsters do not hear much sounds before. Have a nice day.'

'Unnatural sound. What's *that*?' muttered Mat, thumping down the receiver.

'Umn?' said Rod. He was building a statue of a wild boar. It was made from a car sump, a lobster-pot, a traffic bollard, and a basket of huge nails. He was very busy.

'*You're* all right,' said Mat crossly. 'I

come before you in the alphabet. You
have two weeks. I only have one. What
is unnatural sound?'

Rod picked up a bit of copper pipe
which the gas man had given him, and
rattled it along the row of nails on the
back of his boar's neck:

TRR–ING–NG–NG–NG–NG–IIIINNNNGGGG.

'Music,' he said. 'This is where we
have to get together with the Vickers
lot.'

'*Them?* What do they know about
music?'

'Sweet silver nothing. But we'll have
to teach them.'

Rod and Mat went to see their
enemies, the Vickers boys, who, as
usual, were drinking root beer and
playing a game called Drop Dead in
Farmer Gostrey's barn.

'Hey, you dwergs, what you doin''
here?' yelled Ben Vickers, who was the

look-out. 'Frog off! We don't want nothin' to do with you little swickers!'

'Mat this week, ho, ho, Rod next, har har,' shouted Urk over his brother's shoulder. 'Soon the monsters'll have ye. Chomp chomp!'

Urk was the biggest and roughest and toughest of the Vickers boys.

'Yes, and who's the week after? You!' said Rod. 'I've seen old Young's list. He's got your dad down as Mr *Adsett-*Vickers. So you come after us.'

'*What????*'

'Yes! It's so. So listen! We've got a plan. Want to hear it?'

As Rod spoke, a pterosaurus flapped overhead, snapping its razor-sharp jaws. Urk and Ben turned pale.

'Hey, you'd better come in the barn. No sense waiting for an ant bear to come and knock you off. Has old Young *really* got our family down as Adsett-Vickers?'

'Here's the list, look,'

But none of the Vickers boys could read.

'Well, listen. This is what we've got to do,' said Rod. 'We've got to start a band. An Iron Band. A Cast Iron Band. That'll be *really* rough sound. We want to make trumpets, bugles, drums, fifes, cymbals. And we haven't much time to make them. Let alone practise on them.'

'*Practise?*' said Urk, looking disgusted.

But Ben said, 'Hey, our mum's got a set of bagpipes.'

'What'll we make drums *from*?'

'There's an old water tank on wheels in the field behind,' Ted suddenly spoke up. 'Old Gostrey won't kick up if we take it. He got eaten yesterday by an aardvark.'

The tank on wheels, when cut up,

gave them enough metal for several drums, of different sizes. They made bugles from water-sprinklers. The cutting blades of ploughs were rolled up to make trumpets. Old Mrs Abelsea's grannie's warming-pan gave them a fine pair of cymbals. Rod learned to play the bagpipes.

The Vickers boys had never worked so hard in their lives before. As soon as they had real trumpets, bugles, and cymbals to play on, they became as keen as mustard.

Evenings were spent practising in the barn.

Old Mrs Abelsea had a song that she always sang when cutting up carrots.

Skillo-me, skillo-my, throw your peelings
    into the sky,
Skillery-my, skillery-me, throw the rinds in
    the liquorice tree.

It went to a very cheerful tune, so they practised at that. By Saturday, they could all play it pretty well, except Urk, who never came on time.

'But that doesn't matter,' said Rod. 'Just so long as we make plenty of noise.'

On Saturday they started out in a procession round the village green. The stake was already in place, out in the middle. Mrs Vickers had seen to that. And now she was lurking in the phone box, hoping to see Mat tied to it and snapped up by a mammoth.

Plenty of monsters were about. Indeed the music seemed to bring them from all over the district like wasps to jam: giant tortoises, dinosaurs, triceratops, and toothy bat-birds. They hung and trundled and swooped and flapped, they roared and wailed and honked and boomed. More and more came, from further and further away.

But the music was louder than all of them.

'*Give it all you've got, boys!*' yelled Rod, pounding away on his huge drums, and then blowing the bagpipes till his ears stood out sideways. Ben and Len blew trumpets. Urk whanged on the cymbals. Tom screeched on the fife. Ned and Ted were the buglers. Mat had kettledrums and a mouth-organ made from an old toaster, which he played at the same time as he banged his drums.

The noise they made was ear-splitting. Lots of people in the village complained. Mr Young declared that it was an outrage. He was going to write to *The Times*, he said. So did Mr Brook and old Mrs Pinpye.

But Mrs Abelsea said, 'Look, I think some of the monsters are beginning to shrink.'

It was true, they were. Like leaky balloons, they drooped and dwindled. They sighed and sagged. They flickered and flopped. And, at last — by now they were only the size of teacups — they just simply lay down and died.

'Now we've got to bury them all,' grumbled Mr Young.

After that, the boys kept their band going. But they had to find a barn miles and miles away from the village to practise in, because of the complaints from Mr Young and Mr Vickers. (Mrs Vickers, in the phone box, had been sat on by an iguanadon, just before he began to shrink.) And Urk, oddly enough, shrank just as fast as the monsters did, and, in the end, vanished entirely.

Mat rang up Mars to say that unnatural noise had done the job.

'Very happy,' said Mars politely.

'Have a nice day.'

Mrs Abelsea said, 'You see? It all comes of having regular habits.'

This story is by Joan Aiken.

Beauty and the Beast

A very long time ago, in a distant land, there lived a merchant. His wife had been dead for many years, but he had three daughters and the youngest was so lovely that everyone who saw her wondered at her beauty. Her name was Belle, and she was as good and kind a child as any man could wish for. When a storm at sea sank all but one of the merchant's ships, the family was left with very little money, and Belle was the only one of the three sisters who never complained.

'We shall have to clean the house now,' sighed the eldest. 'And cook as well, I daresay.'

'No more pretty new clothes for us,' moaned the second sister. 'And no maid to dress our hair each morning and prepare our baths each night.'

'We are young and strong,' said Belle, 'and we shall manage perfectly well until Father's last ship comes to port.'

'You are a silly goose,' said the older girls. 'Hoping when there is so very little hope. The last ship probably went down with all the rest, taking our wealth with it.'

Spring turned to summer, and towards the end of summer came news that the merchant's last ship had indeed been saved and was now docked in the small harbour of a town not three days' ride from his house.

'I shall set out at once,' he said, 'and return within the week. Fortune has smiled on us at last, and I am in the mood to celebrate. What gifts shall I bring you, daughters, from the grand shops that I shall surely see on my journey?'

'Something that sparkles like a star,' said the eldest. 'A diamond, I think.'

'Something that glows like a small moon,' said the second daughter. 'A pearl to hang around my neck.'

Belle said nothing.

'And you, my little one,' said the merchant. 'What would delight your heart?'

'To see you safely back in this house after your travels would please me more than anything,' said Belle. 'But if I have to choose a gift, then what I should like is one red rose.'

★

As soon as the merchant finished his business in the harbour, he set off for home. His saddle-bags were filled with gold coins, for he had sold everything that had been on board the last of his ships. Even after buying a diamond for one daughter and a pearl for another, there was plenty of money left.

'But,' he said to himself, 'there are no red roses anywhere in the town. I must look about me as I ride, and perhaps I shall see one growing wild.'

The merchant made his way home, lost in daydreams of how he would spend his new-found wealth. Dusk fell and soon the poor man realized that he had strayed from the roadway and that his horse was making its way down a long avenue of black trees towards some lights that were shining in the distance.

'This must be a nobleman's country

estate,' said the merchant to himself. Through tall wrought-iron gates, he saw the finest mansion he had ever laid eyes on. There was a lamp burning at every window.

Having no-one else to talk to, the merchant said to his horse, 'The gentlemen to whom all this belongs is at home, beyond a doubt, and a large party of guests with him, it would seem. Perhaps he will extend his hospitality to one who has strayed from his path. Come, my friend. I will dismount and we will walk together up this handsome drive.'

The gates opened as the merchant touched them. When he reached the front door, he said to his horse, 'Wait here for a moment, while I announce myself.'

He stepped over the threshold, but there was no-one there to greet him, and a thick white silence filled every corner of the vast hall.

'Is anyone there?' cried the merchant, and his own voice came back to him, echoing off the high walls.

He went outside again quickly and said to his horse, 'Come, we will find the stable, my friend, for everyone in the house seems to have disappeared. Still, it is a beautiful place. Perhaps I shall find a maid in the kitchen who will give me a morsel of food and show me a bed where I may spend the night, for we shall never find our way back to the highway in the dark.'

The stable was comfortable and clean, and the merchant fed his horse, and settled him into one of the empty stalls.

Then he returned to the house,

thinking that by now someone would have appeared.

There was no-one to be seen, but a delicious smell of food hung in the air. Yes, thought the merchant, that door, which was shut, is now open, and someone is serving a meal.

He walked into this new room and saw one place laid at a long table. He saw a flagon of wine and one glass, and many china plates bearing every sort of delicacy a person could desire.

'Is there anyone here to join me in this feast?' said the merchant to the embroidered creatures looking down at him from the tapestries on the walls, but there was no reply, so he sat down at the table and ate and drank his fill.

'I think,' he said aloud, 'that I have come to an enchanted dwelling, and I shall now take this candlestick and see what lies upstairs. Perhaps a kind fairy has made a bed ready for me, and a bath as well.'

He went upstairs, and saw that there, too, the lamps had been lit, so that he had no need of his candle. He opened the first door on a long corridor and found himself in the most sumptuous of bedrooms. The sheets were made of silk, and soft towels had been laid out on the bed. He could see curls of steam drifting from an adjoining chamber, and as he pushed open the door, he discovered a bath, ready for him to step into.

'Whoever you are,' said the merchant to the velvet curtains that had been drawn across the windows, 'you are the most thoughtful of hosts. I can smell the lavender oil you have sprinkled in the bath . . . Maybe in the morning you will show yourself and I will be able to thank you properly.'

The merchant bathed and went to

bed and fell into a dreamless sleep.
When he woke up, the curtains had
been pulled back, the sun was shining,
and a tray with his breakfast upon it
had been placed on a small table near
the window. A fine set of clothes had
been prepared for him, and he put it on
and marvelled at how well it fitted. At
first he could not find his own travel-
stained garments, but they had been
washed and dried and pressed and lay
folded beside his saddle-bags, which he
had left beside the front door the
previous night.

'I must go home,' he thought to
himself. 'However pleasant this place
may be, I must return to my children. I
shall fetch my horse from the stable
and set off at once.'

The gardens of the mansion were a
small paradise. Seeing them spread out
before him reminded the merchant that

he still had not found a red rose for Belle.

'In this garden,' he thought, 'there may still be red roses, even though autumn is nearly upon us. I shall pick just one, if I see some, and be gone.'

Flowers still bloomed in the garden, but the merchant had to walk along many paths before he came to a bush covered with red roses, that had just blossomed. He chose the plumpest and smoothest; the most luscious and velvety of all the flowers he could see, and snapped it off the bush.

At that moment, an anguished roar filled the air and there, towering over him, was the most hideous creature the merchant had ever seen; a being from the worst of his nightmares; something that could not be human even though it stood upright and wore a man's clothes and spoke in a man's voice.

'Ungrateful wretch!' this Beast said. 'All that I have done for you: fed you and clothed you and sheltered you ... all that is not enough. No, you must steal a bud from my most precious rosebush. There is no punishment but death for such ingratitude.'

The merchant began to weep.

'I did not mean it as theft,' he said. 'The owner of this place — you — I knew how kind you must be. I thought a rosebud was but a trifling thing after all the wonders you have lavished on me. It is a present for my youngest daughter. I promised her a red rose before I set out on my journey, or I would never have touched anything that belonged to you. I beg you, spare my life.'

'You must not judge by appearances,' said the Beast. 'I love my roses more than anything in the world, and a red rose is no trifling thing to me. Now you have plucked one for your child. I will spare your life, but only on this condition. One of your daughters must return with you in a month's time, and you must leave her here for ever. She must come of her own free will, and bear whatever fate awaits her in this place. If none of your children will make this sacrifice for you, then you yourself must return and be punished for your crime. Go now. I will wait for you and for whichever daughter may choose to accompany you.'

When the merchant reached his home, he wept as he told the story of the enchanted mansion and of what he had promised the Beast. His two elder daughters glanced first at the jewelled necklaces he had brought them and then at one another, but not a word did they utter.

Belle smiled and said, 'Dry your tears, Father. It was for the sake of my red rose that you ventured into the garden, so I shall go with you and with pleasure.'

The cold came early that autumn. As Belle and her father made their way back to the Beast's mansion, snow began to fall, and by the time they reached the wrought-iron gates, it seemed as though white sheets had been spread over the whole landscape. The merchant's heart was like a stone in his breast, and Belle was trying to cheer him as they drew near the house.

'You must not worry about me, Father, for if you do, it will make me very unhappy. I know that my happiness is your dearest wish, so for my sake, let your spirits be high. I want to remember you smiling.' Belle smiled at her father, as if to set him an example. She said, 'This is a very handsome building, and from all that you told me about the Master of this place, he seems to be a kind and hospitable creature. I do not see anything so terrible in living here, if your life is to be spared as a consequence.'

'You have not seen the Beast,' said the merchant, shivering. 'Oh, you will change your tune when you do, my dear.'

The door opened at their touch, just as it had before.

'We have come,' the merchant called out, 'as I promised.'

His words floated up towards the ceiling, but no-one appeared.

'Come,' said the merchant. 'Let us go into the banqueting hall and eat, for we have had a long journey, and you must be hungry, my dear.'

Two places had been set at the table. Belle and her father were eating with heavy hearts when the Beast came silently into the room. It was only when he spoke that Belle caught sight of him, hidden in the shadows by the door.

'Is this the daughter,' said the Beast, 'who comes in your place?'

'Yes, I am,' Belle answered for her father. 'My name is Belle and I am happy to be in such a beautiful house, and happy to be of service to my father.'

'You will not be so happy,' said the Beast, 'once you have looked upon my face. It will fill you with horror and haunt all your dreams.'

For her father's sake, Belle knew she had to be brave. She said, 'I have heard your voice, sir, and it is as low and sweet a voice as any man ever spoke with. Your face holds no terror for me.'

The Beast stepped out of the shadows by the door, and the light of all the lamps in the room fell on his face. Belle's hands flew to cover her eyes, to shield them from the hideous sight, and it was with great difficulty that at last she peeped between her fingers at the Beast.

'Now,' he said, 'are you as ready as you were a moment ago to spend your days with me?'

Belle was quiet for a full minute, then she said, 'I will become used to looking at you, sir, and then I will not flinch as I did just now. You must forgive me for my cruelty. It was the unexpectedness of seeing you for the first time. I shall not hide my eyes again.'

The Beast bowed. 'You are as kind as

you are beautiful. Everything I own, everything in this place is yours to do with as you will. I shall keep out of your sight, except for one hour in the evening, when I will come into the drawing-room for some conversation. For the present, I beg the two of you to enjoy this last night together, for tomorrow your father must leave and return home. I bid you both goodnight.'

The next morning, after her father had gone, Belle wept for a long time. Then she dried her eyes and said to herself, 'Crying will not help me, nor despair. I must strive to enjoy everything there is to enjoy, and find the courage to endure whatever I have to endure.'

She decided to explore the mansion, and found that everything she looked at had been designed to please her.

There were books in the library, a piano in the music room, paints and pencils for her amusement, a wardrobe full of the most beautiful clothes that anyone could wish for, and everywhere invisible hands that made all ready for her and smoothed her way.

Beside her bed, on a small table, there lay a looking-glass and a note which read:

*'Whatever you may wish to see
will in this glass reflected be.'*

Belle picked up the little mirror and wished that she might see her family and know how they fared, but the images that appeared made her so homesick, that at once she put the glass away in a drawer and tried to forget all about it.

And so Belle passed her days

pleasantly enough, and every evening
as the clock struck nine, the Beast
came and sat beside her in the
drawing-room.

At first, Belle dreaded this time, and
the sound of the Beast's footsteps on
the marble floors made her tremble
with fear. But when he sat down, his
face was in shadow, and as they talked,
Belle's fears melted away, and the hour
passed too quickly. Soon, she began to
long for the evening, and to wish that
she might spend time with the Beast
during the day.

One night, as the candles guttered
and flickered, the Beast stood up to
take his leave of her.

Belle whispered, 'Stay a little longer,
sir. It is very lonely and quiet without
you, and this hour is so short.'

The Beast sat down again, and said,
'I will gladly stay for as long as you

wish, but there is a question I must ask you and I shall ask this question every night and you must answer me honestly.'

'I would never lie to you, sir,' said Belle, 'for you are the best and most generous of creatures.'

'Then tell me, Belle, would you consent to marry me?'

'Oh, no, sir!' cried Belle, and her hand flew to her mouth and she shuddered in disgust. 'No, I could never marry you. I am sorry to say this after all your kindness to me, but oh, no, do not ask such a thing of me, I implore you!'

The Beast turned away from the light.

'I apologize for causing you distress,' he said, 'but I must ask this question every night.'

★

Time went by and the Beast spoke of everything: of dreams and songs and poems and flowers and wars and noble deeds and merriment. They spoke of wizards and dragons and magic and marvels, of clouds and mountains and distant empires. They discussed kings and emperors, architecture and farming, families and animals. The only subject they never mentioned was love.

And still, as he left her side, the Beast asked every night, 'Will you marry me, Belle?' and Belle would say that she could not.

At first she said it in words, but gradually, uttering the syllables that hurt the Beast so much began to hurt her, too, and she found herself unable to speak. After that, she simply shook her head and her heart grew heavier and heavier.

One night, after Belle had spent nearly a year and a half in the Beast's house, she took the enchanted mirror out of the drawer, and asked to be shown her family at home. What she saw was an old man lying sick and feverish in his bed. She could scarcely recognize her dear father, who had been so tall and strong and who had seemed to her so young. She wept bitterly at the sight.

'I shall ask the Master to let me visit him,' she decided. 'He would not refuse me such a favour.'

That evening, Belle wept again as she told the Beast of her father's illness.

'If you let me go to him, I promise to come back within the week, only I cannot bear to see him suffering.'

'And I cannot bear to see *you* suffering, my dear one. Take this magic ring with you, and place it on your finger when you wish to return to this place. All you have to do to be in your father's house is look into the mirror and wish yourself transported.'

'Thank you, thank you, dear sir,' said Belle. 'I shall be back with you before you can miss me.'

'And will you marry me, dearest Belle?'

'No, sir,' said Belle. 'You know I could never do that.'

'Then goodnight,' said the Beast, 'and may you find whatever it is you seek.'

The next morning, Belle woke up in her father's house. His happiness at her return was so great that his health immediately improved, and even Belle's sisters were glad to see her. But every night at nine o'clock, Belle found her thoughts turning to the Beast, and she missed their conversations together and their shared laughter.

When the week was over, she was quite ready to leave, but her father's piteous tears persuaded her and she agreed to stay with her family for a few more days. 'The Master will not mind,' she said to herself, 'for he is so kind and gentle.'

On the third night of the second week, Belle dreamed of the rose garden. She saw in her dream the very bush from which her father had taken the red rose she had asked for, and under the bush lay the Master. His voice came to her from far away.

'I am dying, Belle,' she heard. 'Dying for love of you. I cannot live even one more day if you do not come back. You have broken your promise to me, and thus broken my heart . . .'

Belle awoke from the dream at

once, cold and terrified.

Quickly, she put on the magic ring and lay back against the pillows.

'Take me back to him,' she told the ring, and tears poured from her eyes. 'What if I am too late and my Master is dead? Oh, let me be in time. Please let me be in time!'

Belle opened her eyes and she was once more in her bedroom in the mansion. Without even pausing to put slippers on her feet, she ran through the corridors and down the stairs and out of the front door. Breathless, she came to the rose garden, and there on the ground lay the Beast, silent and unmoving. Belle flung herself upon him and took him in her arms.

'Oh, Master, please, please do not die. I cannot, I cannot be too late. How will I ever bear it if you die? Oh, can you not feel my love for you? Come back to life and I will do anything . . . I will marry you gladly, joyously – only speak to me, I beseech you.'

Belle's tears fell on the Beast's hair as she kissed his eyes and clasped him to her heart. At last he stirred and Belle looked down at him for the first time. She found she was embracing a handsome young man, and recoiled at once.

'You are not my beloved Master,' she cried. 'Where is he? I love him. I want to marry him.'

'Don't you recognize me?' asked the young man, who indeed did speak with the Beast's own voice. 'Don't you know me without the mask of my ugliness? It is I, and you will never call me Master again, but Husband and Friend. I am the same as I ever was, and love you as much as I ever did. You have released me from a dreadful spell laid upon me in childhood by a wicked fairy who was envious of my wealth. She turned me into a monster until the day a woman would agree to marry me. Can you love me, Belle, as I really am?'

'I will love you,' said Belle. 'I *do* love you. I have loved you for a long time, though I did not realize it until last night. I love your face, whether it be beautiful or hideous, for it is your face and only an outer shell for your honourable soul.'

'Then we shall be happy for ever,' said the young man. 'And the whole world will dance at our wedding.'

Belle smiled and took his hand, and they entered their home together.

This retelling of a classic fairy tale is by Adèle Geras.

Thing

Emily Forbes and her mother lived in the top flat, and Mrs McIlvray, the owner, lived in the bottom one. Pets weren't allowed in the flats – it was a very strict rule. Mrs McIlvray always stared at Emily severely when they met on the stairs. She looked as though she suspected Emily of smuggling guinea pigs upstairs in her school-dress pocket.

Emily's mother was very understanding. She didn't say irritating things like, 'Never mind, just pretend your nightie-bag pup is a real one.'

Or, 'When you grow up you can have a farm with lots of animals.' She said, 'I just don't know how you can bear it, Emily! It's terrible! I just don't know how you can stand not having a pet!' Which made Emily feel noble and courageous.

It wasn't easy to look pleasant or interested when kids at school talked about their Labrador dog and how he could fetch the morning paper, or their grey Persian cat which let itself be worn as a neck scarf.

A gift shop near her school had pet rocks, with little plastic eyes glued on them, advertised for sale in the window. Having a rock for a pet seemed better than nothing at all. Emily didn't have fifty cents to buy one of the shop-window rocks, so she started inspecting the ground everywhere she went.

Rocks weren't plentiful in that suburb, and the huge ones in the park opposite the flats had been placed there by a crane. Emily knew she wouldn't be able to get one of those up the stairs by herself.

Then one day she found a beautiful rock. It wasn't anywhere special – the bulldozer working on the new sports complex near her school had scooped it up with a load of soil. Emily picked it up and rubbed it clean with the sleeve of her school jumper.

The rock was a cosy, rounded shape, and a gleaming, rich dark brown, the colour of Vegemite in a new jar before anyone shoves a knife in to spread their toast. Emily took it home and put it on the living-room table, propping it up with a lemon squeezer because it was so smooth it tended to roll away.

'Mrs McIlvray couldn't possibly

complain about your keeping a rock for a pet,' said Emily's mother. 'What are you going to call it?'

'I'll call it Thing,' said Emily. 'It's nice and short and easy to remember.' She patted the rock goodnight and went to bed.

Mrs Forbes, who was inclined to be vague about such matters, forgot to turn off the oil heater, and when they got up in the morning the living-room was like a sauna.

'Oh blah!' said Emily. 'The heat cracked Thing.'

'Rocks don't crack as easily as that,' said her mother. 'Let me look.' She picked it up and found that there *was* a crack, like an opening zip-fastener, and while she was looking at it, it zipped open even more. The rock quivered in her hands and made a peculiar slithery noise. Mrs Forbes made a louder one, and dropped it nervously on to the carpet.

Emily was more curious than alarmed, and she poked at the rock with the point of an HB pencil. Something inside tapped back, so she helpfully tugged the two sections of the rock shell apart. A creature wriggled out, uncoiled itself and blinked at them. It was about half a metre long and a most attractive shade of green, like a Granny Smith apple.

'What on earth can it be?' asked Emily's mother. 'I never saw anything like it before!'

'We did a project on dinosaurs at school,' said Emily. 'I think this could be a baby stegosaurus. They weren't as awful as those dinosaurs they have in horror movies, though. I think they were vegetarians.'

'Oh,' said Mrs Forbes, relieved. 'You can give it that left-over coleslaw in the fridge, then.'

'Come along, Thing,' said Emily, and the little stegosaurus followed her into the kitchen. He ate the coleslaw, and four ripe bananas Mrs Forbes was saving to use for banana custard, and half a carton of mango yoghurt. While he was eating, he thumped his tail enthusiastically on the floor.

'If you keep him, you must tie newspapers round his tail to muffle the noise,' said Mrs Forbes. 'It's going to be difficult hiding him from Mrs McIlvray. I think they grow to quite a large size, Emily. Still, I suppose you can deal with each problem as it comes up.'

The first problem for Emily was the worry about Thing being left on his own while she was at school and her mother was at work. Luckily she discovered that he liked television. While she was having her breakfast, she had the set switched on. Thing looked at it with great interest, then he jumped up on the couch and kneaded his little claws in and out of the couch cushions, making a contented purring noise. So Emily left the set turned on, with the sound very low.

When she came home from school, Thing was still on the couch, watching TV. He seemed to have grown a little during the day. Emily fed him a bunch of silverbeet which she had bought at the greengrocer's on the way home.

Mrs Forbes phoned from where she worked, as she did every day to make sure Emily got home safely.

'That stegosaurus should really be getting some outdoor exercise,' she said. 'I don't think dinosaurs just sat around watching TV in prehistoric times. You'll have to smuggle him out into the park, but don't let Mrs McIlvray see you both. And make sure no-one notices you in the park, either, Emily. People can be very mean about animals being a nuisance. They're quite likely to whisk Thing off to a museum and put him in a glass box with a label.'

Thing seemed to understand the need for quiet, even though he was so young. He padded softly after Emily down the stairs, and curled up his tail so that it wouldn't bump from one step to the next.

When it was time to go back to the flat, Thing followed Emily obediently, and she got him upstairs without being seen. But soon there was a knock on the door, and Mrs McIlvray stood outside, looking indignant.

'You've gone and brought a Saint Bernard dog in off the street!' she said. 'The rule here, young lady, is NO PETS!'

'We don't have a Saint Bernard dog,' Emily said truthfully.

'There are large muddy footprints on the steps, and they led right up to this door!'

'Oh, they must be from my new plastic flippers,' Emily said, not so truthfully. 'I was testing them out in the park fountain. I'm sorry, and I'll wipe up the marks straight away.'

'Kindly don't let it happen again,' said Mrs McIlvray.

Emily didn't. She always took two pairs of old woollen socks and put them on Thing before she sneaked him back up the stairs after his daily ten minutes in the park.

Thing was really very little trouble.

He spent all day watching television, with the tip of his tail in his mouth at the exciting bits. He didn't seem to mind what programmes were on. He liked them all: cartoons, classical music concerts, the news and weather forecasts, and even talks on gardening and cookery demonstrations.

At night he slept in a soft bed Emily made from a rubber inner tyre tube she got from the corner garage, and an old duffel coat she didn't wear any more. Thing didn't care that it wasn't a nice, soggy, prehistoric marsh. He circled once or twice then settled down cosily with his nose resting on the tip of his tail.

He had a double row of boney plates down his back, and Emily kept them beautifully polished with Brasso. He grew to about the size of a small rhinoceros, and then stopped growing.

Emily's mother was very relieved.

Thing liked living at Emily's place and being taken for walks. He became very clever at freezing into various shapes when necessary. He could make himself look like an ornamental fence, or a very large cactus on a nature strip. Emily was careful to take him for outings at times when there would be very few people about. The closest he came to being discovered was when they were out skateboarding early one Sunday morning.

They skated up and down the deserted shopping centre. Thing was too large and too heavy to ride the skateboard, of course, but he liked batting it along with his nose while Emily balanced on it.

A group of people from an adult landscape painting class arrived to sketch the buildings. Thing hurriedly

froze into a free-form sculpture in front
of the council library, and Emily sat
protectively on his tail and pretended
to be adjusting the wheels on the
skateboard.

'What an interesting sculpture!' said
the artists, poking at him, and standing
back with their heads on one side,
looking most intelligent. 'How very
modern and unusual. And what
marvellous texture the sculptor
has managed to achieve with
fibreglass!' Emily wished they would
go away.

'It's not a free-form sculpture at all,'
said an elderly woman in a floral
painting smock. 'It's a young
stegosaurus.'

But nobody believed her, and Thing
tried to stay frozen for a long time
while the artists wandered all over the
empty shopping centre practising how

to sketch perspective. He was stiff and creaky as a glacier when Emily was able to take him back to the flat.

'Never mind,' said Emily. 'We'll have a nice little game of kick-the-carton-the-groceries-came-in. Your goal is the couch, and mine's the kitchen door.'

Thing was very good at that game, and he never cheated, either, although he had a tail he could have used, and Emily didn't. The game was very exciting, with five goals each, and they forgot to be quiet. Emily's mother was out, because she sometimes earned extra money at weekends driving taxis, so she wasn't there to remind them about Mrs McIlvray. Soon there was an angry knock on the door.

'Freeze, Thing!' whispered Emily, and he froze into the shape of a coffee-table. Emily reluctantly opened the door.

'I'm sorry about the noise, Mrs McIlvray,' she said. 'I was practising ballet.'

Mrs McIlvray looked past her into the living-room, which had become rather disarranged during the game of kick-the-carton. 'I thought ballet was supposed to be pretty and graceful and quiet,' she said frostily. 'And that is a very odd coffee-table you have there. Made out of green concrete, too. I don't think I can allow you to have concrete furniture in this flat. It might damage the floors.' She came inside and peered critically at Thing, who had his head tucked under his stomach, and his tail tucked under to meet it. 'It's not even very well designed, either,' said Mrs McIlvray. 'I should know, as I collect antique furniture, and I am an expert about good design. What are all those odd flaps sticking up on the

surface? Most illogical, if you ask me!'
She put on her reading glasses to
examine Thing more closely, and
tweaked the blades, along his spine. She
was very surprised when they moved.

'They're specially made like that,'
Emily said quickly. 'They're to hold
magazines and dried flower
arrangements and cups of coffee.'

'I really don't know how your
mother could have bought such a
frightful table,' said Mrs McIlvray. 'Just
look at those heavy thick legs! They'll
wear down the pile on my carpet. You
must tell your mother that this thing
has got to go back to wherever it came
from!'

Thing heard, and was dreadfully
upset. He remembered being in the
rock egg at the sports oval, which
hadn't been nearly as nice as Emily's
place. He unfroze, whimpering, and

scuttled over to Emily and hid his face
in the front of her windcheater.

'It's a sort of mechanical table,'
Emily said desperately. 'It can be used
as a dish-trolley.'

'You naughty little girl!' scolded Mrs
McIlvray. 'You know very well it's a
nasty extinct animal of some kind! I'm
certainly not having a dinosaur living
in my block of flats! It belongs in a
glass case in a museum. I'll give you
until tomorrow night to arrange for its
removal. And what's more, it has to
stay out in the back yard while you're
at school and your mother is at work.
But it has to be gone by tomorrow
evening!'

Emily felt so sad she could hardly
bear it. Her mother, when she came
home, went downstairs to plead with
Mrs McIlvray, but it was useless. They
gave Thing a wonderful feast of every

vegetable and fruit they had in the kitchen, and let him stay up past midnight to watch the late night movie. But in the morning, Mrs McIlvray made them put him out in the back yard.

Emily went to school, crying so hard she had to pretend she had hay fever, and Thing stayed in the back yard. There was nothing happening there except leaves falling from Mrs McIlvray's maple tree, and he wondered why Emily hadn't brought down his TV set and plugged it in. He didn't like being in the yard very much. He chased after the drifting leaves, and played with the handle of the rotary clothes hoist.

Mrs McIlvray came out and scolded him sharply. She wound down the handle so tightly that it couldn't budge, and then she went out shopping. Thing looked wistfully over the front fence, but he knew he wasn't allowed to go out there without Emily to tell him when to freeze.

While Mrs McIlvray was away, a van was driven into the driveway of the flats, and two men got out. Thing quickly froze into something that looked like a length of pebbled patio. The men didn't knock at the door, or open it with a key. Instead, they pulled up the rubbish bin and stood on it and pushed in a flywire screen window to climb into the ground floor flat. Then they opened the door from the inside. After a while they came out carrying Mrs McIlvray's fur coat and her stereo record player and her new electric freezer. They put them into the van and went back inside the flats again.

They came out with Mrs McIlvray's antique oak writing-desk, which was extremely valuable, and her jewel box, and Emily's mother's electric sewing-machine. Thing was delighted to see the sewing-machine being taken away. Emily had to make an apron to pass a school craft examination, and she wasn't very good at sewing. She always looked glum while she was pinning on bias binding, and sewing it, and then unpicking it again because she had sewn it on back to front. Thing didn't like to see her look miserable.

The two men went inside and came out with Mrs McIlvray's antique jade and ivory statues and her nineteenth-century clock, and put them in the van. On their last trip of all they came out with Thing's TV set.

Thing wagged his tail, because he thought these men might kindly plug it in somewhere, and he could watch all the afternoon programmes instead of chasing maple leaves. But they put the TV set in the van with all the other items they had removed from Mrs McIlvray's flat and from Emily and her mother's flat. Then they shut the door of the van.

Thing unfroze a great deal more. He knew that his TV set contained cowboy movies, and yoga five-minute exercises, and How to Grow Better Roses, and Fred Flintstone, and everything he liked to watch, and he wasn't going to let anyone take all that away.

He unfroze completely, went around behind the van, and tried to open the door with his nose. When that didn't work, he stretched out his neck and nudged the two men very politely.

One of them turned ivory and the other one turned jade, just like Mrs McIlvray's antique ornaments, and they leapt into the van and slammed the doors shut. They rolled up the windows at a tremendous speed, sealing themselves in like canned sardines.

They couldn't back their van out into the street, because Thing took up a great deal of space. He sat down and waited patiently for them to get out and unpack his TV set, so they just sat in the van and looked upset and unhappy.

Thing was still sitting and waiting when Mrs McIlvray returned from shopping. At first she looked annoyed to see that he got into her driveway, but then she noticed the broken flywire screen and the van crammed with all her valuable possessions. She dropped her basket and ran down the street to fetch the constable from the police station.

'We've been trying to catch those two burglars for months,' the constable said. 'They're a wicked, scheming, crafty, slippery pair of crooks. I'll take them down to the police station, and then I'll come back for the van. But would you kindly ask your dinosaur to step aside out of the way?'

The two burglars didn't look wicked or scheming when they had to step over Thing's tail and be taken down to the police station – they looked pale and worried.

Mrs McIlvray opened the van door and began to take her antiques inside, and Thing sat very quietly and humbly, with his tail tucked out of the way so he wouldn't be a nuisance. But when Mrs McIlvray finished, she didn't look at him crossly – she bent down and patted him on the head.

'You needn't sit out in the draughty

yard,' she said, 'you can wait in my flat until Emily gets home from school.'

Thing wagged his tail and followed her inside, carrying his TV set in his mouth. Mrs McIlvray plugged it in and switched it on for him. He watched all his favourite afternoon shows, and when there was a demonstration on how to fold origami paper into interesting shapes, Mrs McIlvray even cut up some bright gift-wrapping paper so he could practise. She kept telling him how grateful she was that he had saved all her precious belongings.

When Emily came home, still looking very hayfeverish, Thing was helping Mrs McIlvray unpack her shopping and stack it away in the right shelves. 'I'm sorry he got out of the back yard,' Emily said dolefully. 'And I couldn't find any kid who'd give him a good home. Everyone's mothers said no they couldn't. No-one seems to want a stegosaurus. I guess I'll just have to telephone the museum.'

She couldn't bear to look at Thing. It was heartbreaking to think of your best friend permanently frozen in a labelled glass box. She looked instead at Mrs McIlvray, who was making a very expensive salad of broccoli and eggplant and avocado pear, decorated with little radish roses. Mrs McIlvray put the bowl of elegant salad on the floor in front of Thing.

'Museum?' she said indignantly. 'What on earth are you talking about, Emily? If you don't mind my mentioning it, dear, this dinosaur of yours watches far too much television. It can't be very good for him. While you're at school during the day, I'll

take him for a nice healthy run in the
park – after we've had our lunch.'

This story is by Robin Klein.

Miss Hegarty and the Beastie

When anybody in the village wanted to buy anything at all they went to Miss Hegarty's shop because there was no other shop to go to. The little bell above the door said 'ping!' as soon as the door was opened, and Miss Hegarty came out of her parlour at the back and said, 'Good day to you and what is it you want?' And whatever it was, flour or shoelaces, candles or thread, butter or a mousetrap, Miss Hegarty knew where to look for it. 'And what else do you want?' she asked, and if there was anything else she knew where to find that too. 'Take your time now, don't hurry,' Miss Hegarty always said to her customers, 'I'm sure there is something else you want, and you'll think of it in a moment or two.' And very often that is just what they did. 'If you want it, Miss Hegarty's got it,' they said up in the village.

One evening, just at six o'clock when Miss Hegarty was ready to shut up the shop, she heard the little bell saying 'ping!' but she didn't look up straight away. She was busy counting out the florins and the shillings, the sixpences, the threepenny pieces and the pennies into tall neat piles. But when at last she did look up to see who it was, there was no-one there. So she waited, thinking it was one of the children who was too small to see over the counter. She expected to see a little hand raised and a penny set down, and to hear a voice asking for a gobstopper or a stick of chewing gum. 'Well now,' she said, 'and what is it you want?'

No hand appeared. No-one answered her. So Miss Hegarty leaned across the counter and looked – and she saw the beastie. He was a low, round, fat, happy beastie, and he was lying close up against the counter. The yellow sunlight was shining on him and he had his eyes shut.

Miss Hegarty might have been afraid of a mouse but she wasn't afraid of a beastie.

'Well now,' she said again, 'and what *is* it you want?'

The beastie opened his eyes and looked at her. His eyes were green, like wet green lollipops when the sun shines through them.

'I don't want anything,' the beastie said. 'Thank you very much for asking, I'm sure,' and he closed his eyes again.

'You don't want anything?' cried Miss Hegarty. 'Oh, but you must want something!'

He kept his eyes shut and asked, 'Why?'

'Everybody wants something. That's why they come here. If you open your eyes again and look round the shop you'll soon remember what it is you want.'

He opened his eyes slowly and looked. He looked at the shelves that covered every wall, reaching from floor to ceiling. They were filled with bags of sugar and packets of tea and boxes of buttons and tins of sardines. He looked above his head at the ceiling, which was hung more thickly than any Christmas tree with saucepans, buckets, sausages, shovels and bedroom slippers. He stretched up to look at the counter, packed with postcards, pens, pencils, matches, ink and blotting-paper. He bent down and looked at the floor of the shop where sacks of flour leaned against bags of dog biscuits and bundles of firewood were propped beside a box of oranges.

'Now,' said Miss Hegarty, 'you've had a look. What is it you want?'

The beastie didn't answer, but stared and shrugged his shoulders which were black and shiny, like a plastic waterproof when it has been raining.

'A toothbrush, perhaps?'

The beastie opened his mouth very wide and showed her the large pink cave inside his large pink mouth. There wasn't a tooth to be seen; he couldn't want a toothbrush.

'Shoelaces, then?'

But the beastie stretched out one of his six fat paws (with seven toes on each of them) and there were no shoes, and so no need for any shoelaces.

'Soap?' Miss Hegarty said, but this was a silly question for she could see for herself that he was as clean as if he'd just come straight out of the bath.

Miss Hegarty was puzzled – and cross. She began to guess other things that the beastie might want: 'Scissors; a fourpenny stamp; a packet of cornflakes – I've got some packets with cowboy masks on them; you'd like that, wouldn't you?'

The beastie blew out his cheeks – *pouf!* – and said, 'I've got a face of my own, thank you very much.'

'Of course you have a face,' said Miss Hegarty, 'and a very handsome face it is, too. But there must be something you want. Just stay here very quietly and think of all the things you haven't got; you'll soon find out that you want one of them.'

So the beastie sat very quietly in the sunlight, thinking. Miss Hegarty locked the money in a drawer and pulled down the blinds of the shop and swept the floor. Then she put the brush into the cupboard and came back. 'Well,' she asked, 'and have you remembered?'

The beastie yawned very wide and said, 'I don't want anything at all.'

'This is ridiculous,' Miss Hegarty snapped – she was getting hungry for her tea. 'Everyone who comes here wants something.'

'And when they've got the things they want, what happens next?'

'They soon want other things,' Miss Hegarty said happily.

'And you give them what they want?'

'Oh yes, of course.'

'Dear, dear, just fancy that,' said the beastie, 'and now I remember why I came here. It was because I wanted to.'

'Not to stay!' Miss Hegarty gasped. The shop was full enough already.

'Why yes, to stay!' The beastie smiled. 'Now you mention it, I want to stay very much indeed. That is the only thing I do want. And everyone who comes here gets what they want, you told me that, didn't you?'

'Clever, aren't you?' said poor Miss Hegarty.

'Clever but clean about the house; I always wipe my feet,' the beastie said.

What could Miss Hegarty do? 'You can stay for a week,' she told him. So he stayed for a week. Miss Hegarty built him a little cave of his own in one corner of the shop, out of a couple of deckchairs, six bundles of firelighters, two bags of potatoes and the box of oranges. No-one noticed him, for all the customers were too busy buying what they wanted from Miss Hegarty, and if the shop seemed a little more crowded than usual no-one said anything about it.

At the end of the week Miss Hegarty opened the door of the shop very early in the morning before anyone was about and she moved away the two deckchairs. The beastie was sleeping very peacefully with his cheek in two of his six paws. He opened one eye.

'Now,' said Miss Hegarty, 'you came to visit me because you wanted to, and you have had what you wanted and it is time for you to go.'

'Ah,' said the beastie, 'but wait a bit. There is something else that I want now. You said, didn't you, that there would be something else?'

'You want to go home, is that it?'
Miss Hegarty suggested.

'Not to my home,' said the beastie, 'I want to come and live in your parlour at the back of the shop,' and he looked at her softly and hopefully out of his green eyes. 'Everyone who comes here gets what they want, didn't you say so?'

'Cunning, aren't you?' Miss Hegarty said.

'Cunning but comfortable, thank you very much,' the beastie said.

What could Miss Hegarty do? 'You can stay for a week in my parlour,' she said. So for a week the beastie lived in the parlour at the back of the shop, in a special little corner between the piano and the pot of ferns, and he was very happy, especially when the radio played loud songs. He lay on his back waving time to the music with all six of his paws at once.

At the end of the week, very early in the morning before anyone in the village was about, Miss Hegarty came down to the parlour and moved away the pot of ferns.

'Now,' she said, 'you wanted to stay in my parlour and you have stayed in my parlour and it is time for you to go home.'

'Ah,' said the beastie, 'but wait a bit. There is something else I want. You said, didn't you, that there would be something else? I want to stay for another week and sing to myself. I am tired of the noises that come out of that box.'

'Conceited, aren't you?' said Miss Hegarty.

'Ah, but wait till you hear me singing,' said the beastie.

What could Miss Hegarty do? For a

week the beastie lay in her parlour, singing. Sometimes he sang sea-shanties, and sometimes he sang lullabies; sometimes he sang as loud as a brass band and sometimes he sang as softly as the wind sings on a summer day. The people who came to the shop used to stop halfway down their shopping lists and ask Miss Hegarty what station her radio was tuned in to. Miss Hegarty pretended she didn't hear and hurried on to the next order, and slapped the bags of sugar down on the counter extra hard, to drown the sound of the beastie's voice.

At the end of the week, very very early in the morning, before even the birds were awake, Miss Hegarty went down to the parlour and said to the beastie, 'You wanted to sing and you have sung and now you must stop singing. You must go home.'

'Ah,' said the beastie, and his green eyes shone like traffic lights, 'there is one more thing that I want, just one. I am tired of singing when there is a piano here and no-one playing it. I want you to play for me while I sing.'

'To play for you? How can I play for you when all the people in the village are always coming into the shop wanting things?' she demanded.

'Think of it,' the beastie said. 'They all want things; all day long they want them, from morning to night – pepper and salt, sweets and string, ham, jam, needles and sewing thread; they want different things all the time. But I only want one thing.'

'Well, I don't know—' Miss Hegarty said, and hesitated.

'I do,' said the beastie, and smiled.

So Miss Hegarty sat down on the piano stool and she took some sheets of music from the top of the piano and set them on the music stand and she played – and she played – and she played.

The clock in the village struck nine. People with shopping baskets came to the door but the blind was still down. There were no rows of kettles and buckets sitting out on the pavement, no tin bath filled with bunches of flowers, no box of apples. How very strange! They rattled the door, knocked on the window, stamped their feet, jingled their money, bent down and looked through the slit in the blind and wondered what in the world could have happened.

That wasn't the sound of music they heard, was it? Could it be music? They went round to the garden gate at the side of the shop, and across the garden and then between the flower beds and up to the window of the parlour, and there they stood with their faces pressed close against the glass, gaping. This was where the music was coming from! At the piano, as happy as lords, Miss Hegarty and the beastie were singing duets.

This story is by Janet McNeill.

ABOUT THE ANTHOLOGIST

Pat Thomson was born in Norfolk. She studied French at the University of Leeds and went on to gain further qualifications in library studies and teaching at the universities of Loughborough and Leeds. She has worked as a teacher, lecturer and librarian since then. During her time at home with a young family, Pat became involved with the Federation of Children's Book Groups, for which she is now an Honorary President. Pat was instrumental in founding the Children's Book Award, an annual prize for the best children's book, judged by young readers themselves.

Pat has collected many anthologies of short stories for Transworld, many of which are now classroom favourites. There are individual age-ranged anthologies for children of every age from four to eight and several themed collections, including *A Cauldron of Magical Stories* and *A Bed Full of Night-time Stories*.

Pat now lives with her husband near Peterborough, in a house full of books. She collects antiquarian children's books and babies' rattles, and her husband has an extensive collection of mechanical toys, which sometimes feature in Pat's books. Their two grown-up children have kept up the family tradition and work in education.

Pat regularly visits schools and libraries in her capacity as a children's author, and she frequently contributes articles on aspects of children's literature and reading to specialist journals and magazines.

A PARCEL FULL OF STORIES FOR FIVE YEAR OLDS
Collected by Pat Thomson

Unwrap the parcel and discover a centipede who has a hundred socks (which keep getting lost in the wash), a little boy who wants a woolly mammoth for a pet, and a guinea pig who is teaching himself to read. This is the most exciting parcel you've ever opened!

'Pat Thomson's story collections are always fresh, rich and entertaining'
Books for Keeps

ISBN 0 552 545549

A CAULDRON OF MAGICAL STORIES
Collected by Pat Thomson

Stir this enchanted cauldron and conjure
up ten magical tales — meet hobgoblins,
a bewitched fish, and the last wolf in
England. Read about the fisherman
who sails through the air, the moon that
cannot rise, and the prince who will do
anything for his grumpy princess.

These bewitching stories are by top
authors such as Astrid Lindgren, Kevin
Crossley-Holland and Adèle Geras —
you will be completely spellbound!

ISBN 0 552 545457

A BED FULL OF NIGHT-TIME STORIES
Collected by Pat Thomson

Snuggle up in bed with these wonderful stories. By the light of the full moon, travel on a flying quilt, dance with twelve princesses, or learn how to make a ghost disappear.

Here are tales wrapped in the magic and mystery of night-time from such well-loved authors as Joan Aiken, Helen Cresswell, Dick King-Smith and Philippa Pearce.

ISBN 0 552 529613

A BUCKETFUL OF STORIES FOR SIX YEAR OLDS
Collected by Pat Thomson

Dip into this bucketful of stories and you will find a ghost who lives in a cupboard, a dog that saves a ship, a king who can turn things into gold, a dwarf who becomes a cat, and many other strange and exciting creatures. You won't want to stop reading until you get right to the bottom of the bucket!

ISBN 0 552 527572

A BARREL OF STORIES FOR SEVEN YEAR OLDS
Collected by Pat Thomson

Roll out the barrel and discover
naughty Angela and her sticky school
trick; Frankel, the farmer who outwits
the Czar; Ignatius Binz, a boy with a
truly magnificent nose; a Hallowe'en
trick that goes wrong; and a whole host
of other wonderful characters and
stories. You won't want to stop reading
until you get right to the bottom of the
barrel!

'Lively and rich collections of stories for
all ages' *Books for Keeps*

ISBN 0 552 52817X

A SACKFUL OF STORIES FOR EIGHT YEAR OLDS
Collected by Pat Thomson

Delve into this sack of stories and you will find a Martian wearing Granny's jumper, that well-known comic fairy-tale pair Handsel and Gristle, a unicorn, a leprechaun, a princess who is a pig, and many other strange and exciting characters. You won't want to stop reading until you get right to the bottom of the sack!

'There are thirteen stories to a sackful and each and every one is a tried-and-tested cracker' *Sunday Telegraph*

ISBN 0 552 527300

A CHEST OF STORIES FOR NINE YEAR OLDS
Collected by Pat Thomson

Open up this chest of stories and you will find a starving boy rescued by a cat, a prince who marries a tortoise, a little boy who likes being frightened, kidnappers from space, a bony-legged witch, and many other weird and wonderful characters. You won't want to stop reading until you get right to the bottom of the chest!

'A good mix of stories and styles well suited to the stated age group ... there is something here for everybody'
The Times Educational Supplement

ISBN 0 552 527580

All Transworld titles can be bought or ordered from all good bookshops or are available by post from:

Bookpost
PO Box 29
Douglas
Isle of Man
IM99 1BQ

Tel: +44 (0) 1624 836000
Fax: +44 (0) 1624 837033
Internet http://www.bookpost.co.uk or
e-mail: bookshop@enterprise.net

Free postage and packing in the UK.
Overseas customers: allow £1 per book
(paperbacks) and £3 per book
(hardbacks).